CHRISTMAS AT
HARTFORD HALL

When Elizabeth's grandfather died, there was no sign of a will; and, devastatingly, she discovered she was now dependent on his heir. When the new Lord and Lady Hartford and their twin daughters arrived, they reduced her status to that of a servant. Elizabeth is determined to leave Hartford Hall in the New Year and find work as a governess. But the arrival of Sir James Worthington to make an offer for Lady Eleanor only adds to her difficulties . . .

FENELLA MILLER

CHRISTMAS AT HARTFORD HALL

Complete and Unabridged

LINF✦RD
Leicester

First published in Great Britain in 2011

First Linford Edition
published 2011

British Library CIP Data

Miller, Fenella-Jane.
    Christmas at Hartford Hall. - -
(Linford romance library)
1. Nobility- -Fiction. 2. Grandfathers- -
Death- -Fiction. 3. Love stories.
4. Large type books.
I. Title II. Series
823.9'2–dc22

ISBN 978–1–4448–0691–5

Published by
F. A. Thorpe (Publishing)
Anstey, Leicestershire

Set by Words & Graphics Ltd.
Anstey, Leicestershire
Printed and bound in Great Britain by
T. J. International Ltd., Padstow, Cornwall

1

Elizabeth stepped out of the haberdashers and was almost blown from her feet by a flurry of snow. Botheration! It was more than three miles along narrow muddy lanes to Hartford Hall, she was already tardy, and tramping back through a blizzard would delay her even further.

Mrs Reynolds, the vicar's wife, appeared behind her. 'My dear, surely you are not intending to walk home in this? Come back with me. When the weather improves I shall ask Mr Reynolds to send you back in the gig. Unfortunately he is visiting a sick parishioner at the moment or you could take it now.'

'Thank you, madam, but I must return. Lady Hartford was most insistent that these items were fetched for her this morning. I dare not tarry, the first of the house guests is arriving this afternoon and I still have other duties to perform before then.'

'It's a scandal, my dear, how they treat you up there. Your mother was a Hartford, yet Lady Hartford and her family think of you as little better than a servant. Your dear grandfather would be turning in his grave if he knew.'

Elizabeth's eyes filled at the mention of her beloved grandpa. Until his death two years ago she had been happy, but it had all changed when a distant relative had inherited the title. She was dependent on the new Lord Hartford for everything.

'I must go, ma'am, the longer I stand here the more difficult it will be to negotiate the lanes.' She smiled and tilted her face allowing the snowflakes to fall in her mouth. 'It is going to be a white Christmas, I do so love it when it snows at this time of the year.'

'You're a good girl, Elizabeth. Without your intervention none of the tenants would be living in comfort this winter.' Mrs Reynolds tightened her bonnet strings and nodded. 'Take care, and do hurry. I fear the weather is worsening as we speak.'

Elizabeth put down her heavy basket and pulled her cloak hood more snugly around her head, tied her muffler so that it covered her mouth and checked that her boots were tightly laced. The last thing she wanted was for snow to seep in and soak her stockings before she'd even started her journey. Several townspeople greeted her as she hurried along the pathway. It was always a pleasure to come into Hartford, at least here she was sure of a friendly smile and a kindly word. Several times she was forced to stop and wipe her nose, and her throat was becoming more sore by the minute. Perhaps it would have been wiser to refuse to come out this morning when she knew she had a nasty head cold. She sighed. If she hadn't come then Betty would have been sent instead and she was even more poorly than Elizabeth. It was fortunate the lanes had high hedges on either side as these were preventing the worst of the blizzard from reaching her. Normally she would walk close to the edge just in case a vehicle wished to pass, but today this was all but impossible as the snow was already above ankle height next to the hedge-row.

* * *

James was regretting his decision to drive himself in his new high-perch phaeton to Hartford Hall. The weather, which had been clement when he set out, was rapidly deteriorating. His valet, Duncan, sat shivering on the box beside him, the trunk strapped to the back.

'I fear I have made a disastrous error, Duncan, but it's too late to repine. We must press on. I believe Hartford Hall to be no more than a few miles from here.'

'I think the lanes will be all but impassable soon, sir, and I don't reckon our chances if we were to be marooned in this blizzard.'

'I should never have accepted the invitation, but before I offer for Lady Eleanor I wish to get to know her better, and this seemed an ideal opportunity.'

He flicked his whip in the air to encourage his team; they were not built for such appalling conditions and if he didn't get them into a warm stable soon they might never recover from the experience. His carriage lurched as he expertly turned into the lane that led to his destination.

'Not much further, Duncan. We can increase our speed, there's far less snow on the ground here.'

Suddenly his companion shouted a warning. 'Look out, sir, there's a girl walking ahead of us.' James hauled back on the reins praying he would be in time. The girl wouldn't be able to hear him, the snow deadened the sound of the wheels and the clatter of hooves. To his horror his lead horse was unable to avoid the girl and she vanished beneath the animal. Throwing the ribbons to his valet he leapt from the box and ran to the front of his team. Although the animals were thoroughbred they were not highly strung; they seemed to sense there was someone beneath their feet and were standing quietly.

*   *   *

Elizabeth was lost in thought, recalling two Christmases ago when Grandpa had been well when, seemingly from nowhere, a horse reared up behind her. She had no chance to hurl herself to safety; her last thought as she fell beneath the plunging feet was that she would be with her beloved relative at Christmas after all . . .

Her mouth was full of snow, her basket no longer in her possession, but she was not dead. She daren't move, she was beneath a team of spirited horses, she could be trampled to death at any moment. Then two hands grasped her shoulders and she was hauled backwards through the snow in the most undignified manner and set firmly on her feet. She spat the last of the white stuff from her mouth and glared up into the face of the most attractive man she'd ever seen in her life. He would have been even more handsome if he were not scowling back at her.

'What the devil were you thinking of? I could have killed you. Walking down the middle of a lane is the height of folly.'

This was the outside of enough. The wretched man had all but run her over and was now blaming *her* for his foolhardy actions. 'That I am not dead is no thanks to you. Perhaps it has escaped your attention, sir, but the only place it is possible to walk at the moment is down the middle of the lane.'

He frowned down at her, his startlingly blue eyes unfriendly. 'I do not intend to stand here bandying words with a servant girl, my cattle will freeze.' He raked her with an icy stare. 'As you are obviously unhurt, I shall continue my journey.'

It was only then that she noticed the ridiculous vehicle he was travelling in. She couldn't help herself, her lips twitched and she hastily raised a hand to cover her smile. 'I would think, sir, that driving in the depths of winter in *that* carriage might be considered even more foolish than my walking in the middle of the road.'

She thought he would suffer an apoplexy! His lips thinned and he seemed to grow several inches; now he was even more formidable. His many-caped driving coat was snow-covered, his beaver equally whitened . . . if she thought of him as a rather cross snowman perhaps he would not seem so alarming.

Then his expression changed, his anger gone, and he smiled. My word! He was far more dangerous to her composure when he did this then when he glared at her.

'I beg your pardon, miss, the relief that you were not killed has made me behave appallingly. Although my carriage is not ideal, allow me to give you a ride to your destination. It's the least I could do.'

Flustered by his mercurial change and not quite sure she wished to be squashed between him and his manservant so high from the ground, she shook her head vehemently. 'No, it would be most improper. You continue your journey, I have not far to go, do not worry about me.' She looked around for her basket and spied it at the side of the lane. 'I must recover my purchases, I cannot do so until you have moved away, I believe that most of them are in the snow where I fell.' He didn't offer to assist which was most churlish of him.

'In which case, I shall bid you good day.' He reached into his coat and produced a golden guinea. 'I hope this will be some recompense for the accident.'

He had mistaken her for a servant — probably far better than he knew who she was. Hiding her embarrassment she held out her hand and he dropped the coin into it. On impulse — after all she was supposed to be a member of the lower classes — she curtsied. He nodded and jumped back on to the box. She pressed herself against the hedge and watched his carriage vanish into the whiteness.

She recovered the errant items, brushed off the worst of the snow from her person and was ready to resume her walk. When she turned into the drive a few moments later she was unsurprised to see the imprint of carriage wheels. The handsome gentleman could have been going nowhere else but Hartford Hall. Would he demand his money back when he knew the truth?

★   ★   ★

James could sense the disapproval flowing from his manservant, but the man had more sense than to speak his feelings. It was hardly surprising Duncan was upset, to treat the poor girl so cavalierly beggared belief. What could have possessed him to berate her in that way? And to give her money as if she were a menial, that was equally inexcusable. Everything about the young woman spoke of good breeding. Her clothes were somewhat outmoded but expensive, and her voice that of a gentle woman. Why hadn't she identified herself? The only explanation was that she was a poor relation, or a governess — neither servant nor family, but somewhere in between. But no, the Hartford girls had all come out at the start of this season, there would be no need to employ a governess for them. The girl must be a companion of some sort.

Her hair had been hidden beneath a hideous bonnet, her face besmirched, but he could recall the colour of her eyes exactly. They were dark, not brown, more a violet colour, a most unusual shade. She was above average height, but it had been impossible to see her shape beneath the voluminous folds of her thick cloak. The tip of her nose had been bright red, whether from the weather or a head cold he'd no idea. His mouth curved; he blinked snow from his eyes. One thing he did know was that she was far too light for a woman of her height.

It was likely she was heading for Hartford Hall, he should have insisted that she rode with him, not allowed her to trudge through the snow carrying a heavy basket. He pulled the reins bringing his team to a slithering halt.

'This will not do, Duncan. If the young lady will not scramble up on the box the least I can do is transport her basket for her.'

'Allow me, Sir James. You get the horses in the warm, I'll walk back with the young lady.'

Before he could argue his man

scrambled over the side and disappeared. He must wait until he'd seen to his cattle before offering his humble apologies for his churlish behaviour.

★ ★ ★

Elizabeth had not taken more than a few steps up the drive when an unfamiliar shape loomed through the snow. It wasn't the driver, she would recognize *his* outline anywhere.

'Here, miss, let me carry that for you. Sir James wanted to come himself but I can't handle the ribbons, so I came instead.' The shape bowed and held out his hand for the basket. 'Duncan, is my name, valet to Sir James Worthington.'

She didn't argue. Despite her avowal that she was unharmed by her fall she was feeling decidedly peculiar. No doubt a combination of shock and a nasty head cold was the cause of this.

'I thank you, Mr Duncan, I should be most grateful for your assistance. I don't feel at all the thing, the sooner I get inside in the warm the better I shall be.'

Her throat was too raw to speak further, she must conserve her strength for the long walk down the drive. Halfway along she stumbled to her knees, her head swam, her eyes were blurred. Was she imagining a second figure striding towards her?

'Allow me to assist you, my dear. Good grief! You're burning up, what could have possessed you to go out into the snow with a fever?'

Without a by your leave Sir James snatched her up and swirled his driving cape around her. She felt too unwell to protest, so settled back in his arms with a sigh of relief. It was warm and safe within the folds of his coat, she could feel the thump of his heart beneath her ear, it was regular and steady. He was so strong, what a pity he was such an objectionable gentleman.

By the time they arrived at the Hall she was all but asleep, lulled by his rhythmic strides and the warmth of his body pressed so close to hers. From a distance she heard strident voices, cries and protests, but she kept her eyes closed and held on to his waistcoat tightly. Somehow she knew he would protect her from harm.

* * *

Lady Hartford and her twin daughters were waiting in the vestibule. One would have thought they would have been concerned for the poor girl he carried in his arms but their protests and cries were because he'd had to bother himself in this way.

'Sir James, why are you carrying this person?' Lady Hartford gesticulated to the waiting footman. 'Here, take her to her room, she has caused more than enough trouble for one morning.'

Reluctantly James handed over his burden, although he would not have done so if the young man hadn't looked so stricken. Whatever the Hartfords thought about the young lady, she was obviously well liked by the staff.

'I'll see she is taken care of, sir, you can hand her to me.' The footman's words were too soft for his mistress to overhear.

'See that you do, come and tell me how she does later.'

'Sir James, you are covered in snow. See, it's melting all over the floor. Should you not go upstairs at once and change into something dry? I do not wish you to catch a putrid fever.'

He turned to the girl, smiling down at her disarray. 'I see that you're observant, Lady Eleanor, I shall go at once to my chambers if someone could direct me there.'

She smiled sweetly at him but said nothing further. She looked unhappy about what was being said, but too nervous to speak up.

A short, thin woman with her grey hair scraped back came forward, her navy bombazine rustling as she moved. She curtsied politely. 'Sir James, welcome to Hartford Hall, I shall conduct you to your apartment. I'm Blake, housekeeper here.'

'Thank you, I shall be glad to get into something dry.' On the bottom step of the grand staircase he belatedly remembered the basket Duncan had been carrying. 'Lady Hartford, when I almost ran the young lady down in the lane her basket spilled. My man has taken the items round to the kitchen, I shall make good any discrepancies. Please do not lay any blame on the young lady, it was not her fault.'

Instead of being concerned by his narration the woman pursed her lips and exchanged an angry glance with her daughters. 'Miss Baverstock, a very distant relation of ours, lives here at the generosity of my husband. Therefore she is more than willing to run errands for us and help out in any way that she can. However, I must assure you, Sir James, she is not part of the family. You will not be obliged to sit with her at dinner or dance with her at the Christmas ball.'

A wave of anger almost made him speak harshly. He forced his mouth to smile. 'If you will excuse me, my lady, Lady Amelia, Lady Eleanor, I shall see you later this afternoon.'

He followed the housekeeper along a spacious passageway. 'Where does Miss Baverstock have her apartment, Blake?'

The lady glanced over her shoulder as if concerned she might be overheard. 'She doesn't sleep down here, sir, she lives in the nursery. Don't worry about her well-being, I'll make sure she's nursed back to health. It breaks your heart . . . ' She stopped and flushed painfully. 'I beg your pardon, Sir James, I was speaking out of turn.'

He nodded and no more was said. Duncan was awaiting him, a hot bath had been drawn and fresh garments laid out in the commodious dressing room. James knew that his man would soon discover what it was the house-keeper hadn't told him about Miss Baverstock's position in the family.

As he relaxed in the warm water he

thanked God that Eleanor was not of the same ilk as her sister and mother. However, it was strange that his intended beloved had never mentioned having a distant cousin living with them, especially as she must be about the same age as her.

2

'There you are, Miss Baverstock, you'll feel more the thing when you drink this tisane that Cook has prepared for you. It will ease your sore throat and help you sleep.'

Elizabeth accepted the hot drink gratefully. 'Thank you, Mrs Blake, you are all so kind to me and I don't deserve it.'

'That you do, my dear, we've watched you grow up. It's criminal how you're being treated now when this has been your home since you were in leading strings.'

This was a familiar topic of conversation and one with no future in it. 'Mrs Blake, I beg you not to keep reminding me how things were. I must be thankful that I have a roof over my head. Poor Grandpa was taken so suddenly he had no time to arrange a settlement for me.

I must make the best of things. At least I'm still living in the house I love so much.'

Mrs Blake snorted but said nothing further on the subject. 'Sir James, who carried you home, is most concerned about your welfare. George is to tell him how you fare.'

'I've finished, Mrs Blake, thank you. There's a good fire in the grate and with the curtains drawn I shall be perfectly snug. Please do not trouble yourself to be running up and down after me, I have a jug of lemonade and that is all I require at the moment.'

The housekeeper bustled off and Elizabeth settled down in the narrow bed. Lady Hartford had refused to allow her to exchange it for something bigger, it was meant for a child and her long limbs were difficult to organise comfortably. If two of the footmen had not moved the bed against the wall no doubt she would frequently fall out on to the boards.

In spite of the sparseness of her

accommodation she was content up here away from the constant criticisms and sharp reminders that she was no more than a drain on their resources. Sometimes Eleanor crept up to be with her, although not often — she was too afraid of her mother and sister to risk being discovered where she ought not to be. However, knowing that not all the family hated her was a great comfort in the dark hours of the night.

As she was drifting off to sleep something Eleanor had told her when she had returned from Town last week popped into her mind. A Sir James Worthington was coming to stay for the festivities and he was expected to make her an offer. Could the gentleman who'd done his best to kill her in the snow be the very same person? If it was he, then he was not right for Eleanor. He was too forthright, too dictatorial, would scare his would-be bride into accepting him. He must be an eligible *parti*, a wealthy man of impeccable breeding, Lord and Lady Hartford would consider no less for either of their beautiful daughters.

He would be more suited to Amelia, she was as sharp as her mother and would not take kindly to being dictated to by anyone. Indeed, she was her papa's favourite, the older of the two by a few minutes only, but one would think she was her sister's senior by several years at least. It would be interesting to watch from the sidelines, although she was rarely asked to dine with the family. She preferred to eat her meals in the kitchen or on a tray up here. When she was obliged to sit at the table in order to make up the numbers she was either ignored by the family or constantly reminded of her good fortune to be living at Hartford Hall when she was destitute.

With so many guests expected over the next two days there would be no need for her — the enormous table in the formal dining room would be quite full enough. She had often slipped in to the grand drawing-room and hid herself behind a convenient pillar in order to listen and observe on similar occasions. She had every intention of doing so this time.

★ ★ ★

'Duncan, what can you tell me about Miss Baverstock? It's quite plain that she's taken advantage of here, but then that's often the case with a poor relation.'

'It ain't like that here, sir. Everyone below stairs is only too happy to tell me of the iniquities of your host and hostess. Miss Baverstock has lived here since she was a tot, when her grandfather died sudden like. He'd made no financial provision for her so she's obliged to suffer or be on the streets.'

James threw down his riding crop, barely restraining himself from cursing volubly. 'Where did these current incumbents come from? I cannot believe they were always living in such

24

style, or had so much wealth at their disposal.'

'You have hit the mark, sir, with that. The present Lord Hartford had no expectations of inheriting, was living as a country squire in Bedfordshire. He was discovered by the lawyers, it seems there is a direct line through a great uncle, but he's not born and bred to this.'

'Small wonder they wish to keep her away from their guests, she is as different to their girls as chalk is to cheese. Her gentility and refinement do not show the others in a good light.'

He frowned, he should not be discussing such matters with his valet, he must be more careful what he said in future. Quickly changing the subject he enquired about the other guests.

'How many are expected? I heard at White's that Lord Bloomfield is coming with his entire family. Hasn't he got two sons and two daughters all of marriageable age?'

'He's to have the apartment next to

this, his progeny are on the other side of the house. From what I heard there will be thirty staying here, but I don't believe any other of them are likely to be known by you, Sir James.'

'I like Bloomfield. At least I shall have someone to play billiards with when I wish to escape from the ladies.'

He was conducted through the splendid building by a footman who had been assigned to him for the duration of his visit. He was delighted to see it was the same young man who had carried the patient away.

'How is Miss Baverstock? What did the physician say when he called?'

'He wasn't sent for, Sir James. Mrs Blake is good with fevers and such, she'll get better treatment from her anyway.'

'Can you arrange for the basket of fruit in my room and the flowers to be transferred to Miss Baverstock, with my compliments?'

The footman beamed. 'I'll see to it myself, Sir James. Lady Hartford says I am to fetch and carry for you so they can have no objection.'

Downstairs there was a confusion of new guests. Lady Hartford and her daughters were greeting each one in turn, but of Lord Hartford there was no sign. This was a further indication that the newly elevated peer did not know the correct way to behave. Not wishing to be involved with introductions, James slipped past unnoticed and strolled into the grand drawing-room, as it was called.

It was certainly large enough to be the main reception room, but grand it certainly wasn't. He shuddered at the black and gold furnishings. Her lady-ship was obviously a slave to fashion, and every item of furniture reflected the Egyptian theme. It was not in keeping with the elegant proportions of the room. No doubt what had been here before was now consigned to the attics along with poor Miss Baverstock. The patter of slippers alerted him and he glanced over his shoulder. 'Lady

Eleanor, I am delighted to see you again. It has been too long since we met at the Cavendish party last month.' She curtsied and he bowed, but somehow he didn't think she enjoyed him kissing her hand.

'Sir James, I've been so looking forward to your visit. Mama says I am to apologise on her behalf that you were obliged to become involved with Elizabeth. Mama is most annoyed with her.'

'Unnecessary, my dear, I did no more than any other gentleman would do for a lady in distress.'

'Do you know I'm not allowed to go up and see how she is? She's the dearest girl, I don't understand why Amelia and my parents have taken such a dislike to her. The staff treat her with the utmost respect, which is something I suppose.'

He smiled warmly at the girl he'd all but decided to propose to this holiday. 'I'm happy that you do not share their feelings, my lady. I understand that

Miss Baverstock has lived at Hartford Hall since she was very small, it must be hard for her to be excluded from the family in this way.'

'I'm certain that it is, but she has nowhere else to go and Mama says that being the granddaughter of an earl is not sufficient to attract a husband. Without countenance and fortune I fear she is stuck here unless she cares to take employment as a governess or companion.'

'Whatever Lady Hartford says, Lady Eleanor, it would be most unsuitable for Miss Baverstock to be obliged to work for her living. *Her* pedigree is impeccable.' The girl's face crumpled at his sharp retort. He must remember to speak softly to her, she was of a nervous disposition and easily upset. 'I beg your pardon, my dear, for speaking so abruptly. Come, I should like to see around this excellent building. Will you be my guide?'

★ ★ ★

When Elizabeth woke up the next morning she felt considerably better, quite well enough to get up and resume her normal chores. If she was honest she much preferred to be busy, working with those who loved her, not sitting about in idleness all day as the family did.

She scrambled out of bed unsurprised that no one had found time to come up and light her fire. They would be far too busy with all the Christmas guests who would have arrived by now. The sun was shining through the frosted panes. She breathed on the glass to clear a space, and her spirits lifted. It was so beautiful, the trees sparkling, the grass a carpet of white upon which black footsteps could be spied. Someone was up before her, already out for a morning constitutional.

The mantel clock showed there was ample time for her to break her fast before supervising the collection of the greenery to decorate the house. A huge tree trunk had already been placed in the massive fireplace in the entrance hall. This Yule log would be lit on the day of the ball and would then burn throughout the twelve days of Christmas.

There was little point in lighting a fire in her bed chamber now, she would dress and go straight to the breakfast parlour. It would be warm in there. Having scrambled into her underpinnings she selected a warm, blue velvet, long-sleeved gown from her closet and hastily stepped in to it. When Lady Hartford had insisted she wore her hair under a cap it had been her intention to conceal Elizabeth's true appearance. However, Sally — who had once been Elizabeth's abigail but now attended to Amelia — had made her half a dozen caps from antique lace and although these were hardly flattering, they were not as bad as they could have been. The fact that they covered up her hair was also an advantage, she had no wish to attract the attention of any visiting gentlemen.

Several servants enquired solicitously after her health and she was happy to reassure them that her sojourn in bed had fully restored her. As expected it was far warmer downstairs than in her own accommodation, she didn't really require her wrap but as she was going to be outside directly after she'd eaten, she kept it with her. She was already wearing her stout walking boots under her gown, not appropriate, but as she was all but invisible to anyone apart from the staff it was of no account. She walked straight into the breakfast room heading for the sideboard upon which were the usual dozen or so silver servers all filled with appetising items. Her stomach gurgled loudly. Most days she had little time to eat, and even when she did her appetite was not what it used to be. She was in the process of examining the contents when someone spoke behind her.

'Allow me to serve you, Miss Baverstock, I've finished my repast.'

Her shock at seeing Sir James

standing behind her caused her to inadvertently drop the heavy silver lid. It landed squarely on his booted toe. His exclamation brought colour to her cheeks. She'd never thought to hear such language in the house.

'I do beg your pardon, Sir James, but if you will creep up on a person in that way you have only yourself to blame if something is dropped upon your toe.' Whatever had possessed her to say that? She hadn't felt so animated since Grandpa had died, but she would have done better to apologise unreservedly. If Lady Hartford were to hear of her pertness she would be locked in her rooms without food or water, as had happened several times before she'd learned to hold her tongue.

To her surprise he took no offence. Instead he grinned. 'And I beg *your* pardon, Miss Baverstock, for using such language in your presence and also for startling you.' His eyes twinkled wickedly as he continued, 'I believe you did not hear me because of your hunger.

Now, the matter is settled, will you allow me to fetch your breakfast?'

How could he mention such a thing? The rumbling of her insides was not a suitable subject to be discussed between a lady and gentleman. 'No, thank you, sir. I'm quite capable of fetching my own breakfast.' His eyebrows almost shot beneath his hair. Oh dear! She tried to retrieve the situation by a winning smile, it did not succeed. 'I should like some coffee, perhaps you would care to pour me some?'

Frostily he nodded. 'I shall not discommode you further, madam. I shall leave you to eat in peace.' He strode out, back ramrod stiff, more than two yards of deeply offended manhood. Shrugging philosophically she returned to the food and piled her plate with a little of everything. She was about to begin her repast when the door opened and Sir James stepped in. To her astonishment he winked at her and then solemnly poured out two cups of coffee and brought them across.

'Do you prefer to drink it black, or would you like me to fetch you cream?'

'I like it black, it's a wonderfully restorative drink, don't you think, Sir James?'

He pulled out a chair directly opposite to her, sat and then smiled. Her heart somersaulted. What was it about this man that made her feel so peculiar, forget her manners and behave quite out of character?

'Miss Baverstock, shall we start again? It was most unfortunate beginning to our friendship. I cannot think why I stormed off in high dudgeon, I'm normally an even tempered gentleman. So for a second time I beg your pardon for my ill manners.'

She could not eat with any degree of enjoyment with him watching her every movement. She had been looking forward to this meal, and however charming this gentleman was her need to eat substantially was far more important.

'Please do not be offended, Sir

James, but I find it impossible to enjoy my food with someone watching my every mouthful. I have yet to thank you for carrying me home yesterday . . . '

He stood up and bowed. 'There's no need, you would not have been in such a predicament if I had not run you down. I fully understand your wish to eat in peace. I should like to talk to you again however. Shall you be around later this morning?'

'I have tasks to perform, Sir James. I must organise the collection of the necessary greenery to decorate the house, I expect it will take me most of the day.'

'In which case, I shall leave you. No doubt we shall meet again soon.'

The door closed and the room felt strangely empty without him. This would not do, he was Eleanor's intended, she must not think of him this way. Anyway, why should he be interested in her when he could marry a beautiful, titled young woman who brought with her a substantial dowry.

Eleanor and Amelia were not identical twins, in fact they could not be more different in personality if they tried. Whereas Amelia was sharp tongued and quick to find fault, just like her mother, Eleanor was quiet and kind. Who she took after was a mystery. Certainly not her papa, who had neither of those qualities. In appearance the girls were similar. Both had abundant nut-brown hair, hazel eyes and well rounded figures. They both dressed to advantage, but Elizabeth was not surprised it was Eleanor Sir James preferred. She would be more biddable, far less likely to gainsay him.

Her appetite had deserted her. She forced herself to consume a quarter of what she taken but it did not settle well in her stomach. Since her life had been turned upside down two years ago her digestion had become a problem. She was certain it was because of the constant agitation caused by the friction between herself and the new incumbents. This would be the last

Christmas she would spend at Hartford Hall. In the New Year she would start her employment as a governess. She had seen the advertisement in The Times and written several weeks ago. On the pretext of saying she was visiting her own ex-governess, she escaped for three days to London where she met her prospective employers.

She was amply qualified, spoke both Italian and French fluently, could play the pianoforte and paint a pretty watercolour, all prerequisites of the kind of employment she sought. The fact that she could also teach Latin, mathematics and world geography was the deciding factor in being appointed, despite her inexperience. She would not reach her majority until next November, but Lord and Lady Bath had been sufficiently impressed with her to decide to overlook her lack of years. Their progeny were all under ten years of age, so to them she would seem mature, and she was looking forward to beginning her new life. The past two years had been miserable. There was nothing worse than being an outcast in one's own home.

Pushing her plate aside she drained her coffee and returned upstairs to put on her outer garments. She stopped, and her eyes widened when she saw what had appeared in her quarters. A large basket of hothouse fruit and an elaborate arrangement of flowers from one of the heated greenhouses, was standing on the old pine table that had once been used as a desk.

There was no note, but she knew at once from whom they'd come. It could be none other than Sir James who had sent her up the gifts that had been given to him by his hostess. It was so kind of him, she was a perfect stranger and yet he had thought of her well-being. She blinked back her tears. It had been so long since anyone had thought to give her a gift of any sort.

The rich aroma of a pineapple restored her appetite and by the time she had devoured half of it, she was tardy. She had no wish to keep the half a dozen outside men who were to accompany her waiting in the cold. It was her task to find suitable mistletoe, holly, ivy and any other evergreens in the dense woodland that surrounded the park. A cart was to accompany them, and it would need to be filled to capacity in order to decorate all the main reception rooms.

This was a task she relished and one that Lady Hartford had been glad to delegate. She'd even agreed to order the extra beeswax candles and the many yards of red, green and gold ribbon that would be needed to achieve the appropriately festive look. A sack of fir cones had already been collected, and these would be arranged in baskets and put on suitable surfaces.

Outside it was crisp and dry, the blizzard long gone, just a thin coating of snow left behind. She joined the group of men waiting by the cart. It was only then she saw another party approaching. Sir James had brought along Eleanor, Amelia and two unknown gentlemen — and here *she* was wrapped up like a woolly parcel.

3

James had little difficulty in persuading the two Bloomfield boys to accompany him in a search for greenery. They were as eager as he to stretch their legs and work off the enormous breakfast they had just eaten.

'Sir James, are you going out?'

He swallowed his smile. For all her sweetness of nature Eleanor was not especially quick of intellect. 'Indeed we are, Lady Eleanor. Why don't you accompany us? We are going with Miss Baverstock to collect festive greenery. It's many years since I was involved in such a pastime and Mr Bloomfield and his brother are to come too.'

Her brow creased as she considered his invitation. Then Ned Bloomfield, the eldest boy, turned to her. 'Please, do come, it will be a lark. It's ages since I've built a snowman, won't you help us do that after we finish collecting in the woods?'

She blushed prettily and smiled up at him. 'Then I *shall* come. Elizabeth will be glad of my company I'm sure.'

Whilst they waited for her to run upstairs and put on what was necessary Ned turned to him. 'I say, Sir James, what a pretty girl, and so sweet. I can't remember when I was more taken with a young lady.'

'Unfortunately, sir, she is almost spoken for. I have been invited to spend the festive season here in order for us to become better acquainted.'

The young man turned an unbecoming shade of puce, tugged at his neck cloth as if it were strangling him and mumbled an incoherent apology. It was a relief when Eleanor appeared after an awkward ten minutes. However, this turned to dismay when James saw that her unpleasant sister had decided to join them on this jaunt.

'La! Sir James, I could not allow all of you to go out in the snow without me. I am an intrepid walker, as everyone will confirm, and there's nothing I like better than to be outside doing something useful.'

'We are delighted you have decided to accompany us. The more there are to help the sooner Miss Baverstock shall be able to get back into the warm and take care of her cold.'

Amelia's smile slipped at the mention of this name. He wished his words back but it was too late, the damage was done. He saw her take hold of her sister's elbow and pull her to one side. He could not overhear the whispered conversation but from the distress on Eleanor's face she was being taken severely to task for involving any of the guests in an expedition that included the unwanted relative.

He was at a loss to know why he was so concerned for this young woman's welfare. It was hardly for her beauty; apart from her eyes she had nothing to recommend her. And it was certainly not for her accommodating nature, she was not in any way submissive but rather of quick intelligence and fiery temperament.

'If everyone is ready we must depart. I believe a cart is to accompany us and it never does to keep a horse waiting, even one that is bred to work.'

A chorus of agreement greeted his suggestion, even Amelia acquiesced and began a lively conversation with Ned Bloomfield. He could not help but notice Eleanor's crestfallen expression as her sister pushed her arm through Ned's and marched him out through the door. He hung back watching Eleanor, her eyes following the young man as he bounded down the steps like an overeager puppy. Why did she not look at him in that way? If he was not careful he would lose his sweet young thing to another suitor.

★ ★ ★

'Eleanor, Amelia, gentlemen, I had no idea you intended to come with me this morning, but you are most welcome. I hope you are wrapped up warmly, it will be decidedly chilly in the woods.'

Amelia stared at her through narrowed eyes and hissed, 'I shall take charge of this venture, Elizabeth. In fact, as you are suffering from a head cold, why don't you return to the house and leave the matter to us?'

If she had been offered the opportunity to avoid this task a quarter of an hour ago she might have accepted, as her pleasure in the excursion had waned when she'd realise just how cold it was. For some perverse reason though, now that others were to accompany her it no longer seemed like a penance but a treat. 'I thank you for your consideration, Amelia, but I am fully recovered and looking forward to doing this.'

'Then you may walk with the gardeners. Do not think to intrude where you're not wanted or it will be the worse for you. Remember your position. One word from me and you will be homeless.'

Elizabeth's happiness faded; why did Amelia always have to spoil everything for her? Well, it was no use railing against fate, she supposed. She'd had eighteen years of comfort and happiness, she must consider her blessings and not dwell on such matters. She had a roof over her head, clothes on her back and sufficient food to eat, far more, in fact, than a lot of the poorer folk in town. Next week she would begin a new life away from here and Amelia's taunts would no longer hurt her.

She fell back to walk among the outside men who greeted her with enthusiasm. The head gardener, Bert Smith, pointed to the cart with a grin.

'Why don't you hop up on there, miss, there's a pile of sacks to sit on and a rug to put over your knees. You still look a mite poorly, don't want to overdo it not with all them guests to see to.'

'I shall do that, Bert, it's a long time since I've stolen a ride in a diligence.' She scrambled up and made herself comfortable inside. It was far warmer snuggled up than it had been trudging through the snow.

'Here, miss, they ain't going in the right direction. Shall we follow them?'

She sat up and peered over the edge of the cart. Sure enough Amelia was leading them away from the best place to find holly with berries on. She should call them back, tell them they were incorrect but some imp of mischief held her back.

'No, Bert, we shall continue as planned. No doubt at some point someone will notice that our vehicle is no longer following them. I expect they will have had enough very soon and wish to return to the house leaving us to get on with our job without interference.'

★   ★   ★

'Sir James, look, the cart is going in a different direction from us,' Eleanor said quietly.

James glanced over his shoulder and saw that she was quite correct. What was Miss Baverstock playing at? It was one thing to play a trick on Lady Amelia, but quite another to involve her sister in such a stratagem.

David Bloomfield shouted after his brother who was marching gaily ahead with Amelia hanging on his every word. 'What ho! Ned, we're all going the wrong way it would seem. Tally ho! We must run to catch them up.' He set off at a spanking pace sending clouds of snow in all directions.

The couple turned and holding hands ran across the park diagonally, they would reach the cart first. This would not do, he couldn't let the young striplings beat him. 'Come along, my dear, we must join the race.' Laughing he grabbed her hand and prepared to set off.

'Please, Sir James, I do not care to

run; I beg you, let us walk quietly.'

Her little face was screwed up with anxiety, and he had not the heart to insist. 'Very well, my dear, we shall not join in their antics but behave like adults.'

He watched the other three laughing and calling out like children. It was a shame his partner had not wished to join in the game. It was a long time since he'd played the fool. They were greeted by the gardeners, and the figure on the cart, with shouts of encouragement.

'My dear, do you not like to have fun? Surely you are too young to wish to give up such frivolity?'

She smiled sweetly up at him, apparently unaware that he was disappointed by her lack of enthusiasm. 'Oh, Sir James, I have never liked frivolity of any sort. I am of a serious turn of mind, and until today I had no idea my sister would enjoy such silliness. I did not think that Mr Bloomfield was a gentleman of *that* sort.'

'He is a young man full of energy, one would not expect him to be staid.'

'Of course not, sir, I much prefer an older, steadier gentleman. That is why I have so enjoyed your company these past weeks.'

Good gracious! To be thought of as already past his prime when he had not yet reached his thirtieth birthday was doing it too brown. The others had joined the cart and there was a lively game of snowballing taking place between the four of them. This morning was a revelation. Amelia had proved herself to be full of fun and Eleanor . . . well, she was old before her time. A pretty young thing like her, scarcely out of the school room, but already wishing to be quiet and serious. But hadn't these been the very qualities that had attracted him? He shouldn't cavil when his choice of bride behaved in exactly the way he expected her to. At least he no longer had to worry about the older Bloomfield lad cutting him out, he was more likely to make a match of it with

Amelia judging by the squeals and giggles coming from this girl.

★   ★   ★

A shout attracted Elizabeth's attention. To her amazement it was Amelia and Ned Bloomfield racing towards her, hotly pursued by the younger brother. Sir James and Eleanor were walking sedately, so it would be some time before they caught up with the cart.

For the first time in ages she felt a surge of excitement. Tossing aside the rug she started to gather up balls of snow. It was her turn to join in the fun! To be part of this escapade lifted her spirits, made her feel that this Christmas might be happier than she could have ever hoped for.

Crouching down behind the protection of the cart side she hurled the first missile, it was a hit direct knocking Ned's hat to the ground. His look of comical disbelief made her laugh out loud. She sent a second snowball hurtling towards Amelia hitting her squarely on her chest.

Both of them screamed a challenge and began scooping up snow to throw at her. She had the better of it being able to hide behind the edge of the cart, but there were now three of them aiming at her and they were closing in. Should she surrender or fight to the bitter end?

'We have you now, Miss Baverstock, you shall get your comeuppance.' Ned appeared at the open end of the vehicle and enormous snowball in his hand.

Without hesitation she hurled her final missile hitting him full in the face, her shout of triumph was short-lived as Amelia and David appeared on either side of the cart and bombarded her mercilessly with snow. Spluttering and laughing she gave in.

'I am beaten, you are the winners of this fight.' She stood up and shook off the snow amidst the laughter. She waited for Amelia to return to her sniping, but the girl, her face flushed and her eyes sparkling, scrambled up beside her on the cart.

'Elizabeth, I've never had such fun. Do you mind if I ride with you? I fear all that exercise has quite fatigued me.'

'Please do, you're very welcome. I fear your bonnet will never be the same. I have had the best of it being dressed like a scarecrow.'

'Never mind, no one is going to notice you anyway.'

Things had not changed between them, not really, Elizabeth realised. It was a truce, a cessation of hostilities — even Amelia knew that being unkind would not impress the gentlemen.

'I say, Miss Baverstock, why did you abandon us?'

'Mr Bloomfield, it is I who have the task of collecting greenery, you are merely out for a walk. The holly trees with the most berries are just ahead, in the next stretch of woodland. Where you were heading is mostly oak, chestnut and ash, none of them suitable for decorating the Hall.'

Five of the outdoor men walked ahead with shears and blades to begin the arduous job of cutting tree branches. The remaining man plodded along beside the cart horse. He glanced sideways as Elizabeth resumed her seat on the sacks and grinned at her. She smiled back. He appeared as pleased as she that at last she was being included by the family that had taken over her home.

Amelia was chatting animatedly to Ned, and David joined in. Once more Elizabeth felt herself invisible. Sir James caught up with them and tenderly lifted Eleanor on to the cart. She remained with her feet dangling over the end and made no attempt to crawl backwards and sit on the sacks. He strolled down the unoccupied side until he was level with Elizabeth.

'Miss Baverstock, I shall no longer fret about your health. You are obviously fully restored, judging by the vigorous defence you put up just now.'

'I thank you for your kind thoughts,

Sir James, and I also thank you for sending me the flowers and fruit. I should have been away before your party came out if I had not delayed to eat half a pineapple.'

His eyes were friendly as he smiled. He was indeed a most attractive gentleman when he put himself out to be charming. 'Do you arrange the decorations yourself, Miss Baverstock, or do you merely direct the operation?'

'A little of both. It would not be possible to achieve the result I wish for if I left things entirely to the staff. However, I must assure you, that this is one task that I relish. It has always been a pleasure to see Hartford Hall dressed for the Lord's name day, it's a tradition that goes back many years.'

'If you require extra assistance, I'm sure we should all like to help. I can remember helping my mother, when I was a boy, to do the same thing. It would be most enjoyable to be able to be involved again after so many years.' His expression darkened as if thoughts of his past were not pleasant. Her heart went out to him, she hated to see anyone unhappy.

'I should be honoured if you would care to help me. It will make the task much easier having someone knowledgeable at my side.'

Amelia overheard this conversation and her head snapped round, her eyes sharp, no longer feigning friendship. 'Sir James, Elizabeth prefers to work alone. This year Mama has kindly allowed her to arrange the greenery in the way it was done before we arrived.' She smiled coldly at Elizabeth before continuing. 'However, this changes everything. Now Elizabeth is prepared to allow others to help, it's no longer her prerogative. I shall direct operations.'

His stare was arctic. 'Let us hope, Lady Amelia, that your efforts to take charge of this matter are more successful than you were when leading us to the place where the greenery is growing.'

Amelia flushed, but did not back down. It was not in her nature to apologise or admit that she was wrong. 'How could I be expected to know where such things grow? After all it is not I that have lived here all my life.'

Elizabeth held her breath, this was the first time this fact had ever been aired in public. The whole family went to great lengths to keep her past a secret. Amelia's embarrassment had caused her to inadvertently reveal this information. Sir James glanced in her direction and something flashed in his eyes, but then he turned back to Amelia.

'Exactly so, Lady Amelia. No one should ever forget that Miss Baverstock is the granddaughter of an earl, was born and bred here, and is a true aristocrat.'

What he left unsaid was more potent than his actual words. Even Eleanor was shocked by his directness. She spun round, mouth open, to stare at him. It was Ned who broke the silence.

'I say, when Pa said we were to come here for Christmas I'd no idea I should be meeting so many lovely young ladies. What a lucky fellow I am to be sure.'

David immediately chimed in. 'I shall ask all of you to dance with me at the ball next week. I've been learning how to waltz, do you think your parents will allow us to do this new dance?'

Elizabeth waited for Amelia to disabuse the young men, tell them in no uncertain terms that she was not invited to the ball. Her role would be to oversee the preparations and then retire to her chambers and then she must be up at dawn to make sure the servants put the house to rights before the guests got up. Her anguish must have shown in her expression, for a strong hand gripped her shoulder for a second to reassure her. 'And I shall do the same. In fact it will be my absolute pleasure to stand up with each of you in turn.'

She sank back against the cart side. Sir James's comment meant that even

Lady Hartford could not prevent her appearance. Amelia laughed.

'Of course Elizabeth shall be there, I'm sure we all cannot wait to see what delightful ensemble she appears in.'

Elizabeth clenched her hands, her momentary happiness squashed. She had nothing to wear, had never owned a ball gown, indeed had never even been to a formal dance. She would look an antidote, would have to appear in an outmoded evening dress. Amelia's triumphant smile, before she turned to continue talking banalities with the Bloomfield gentlemen, reinforced her misery. Whatever the provocation she would not attend. She would rather miss this event than become a laughing stock and bring shame on her dear, departed relative.

4

Scarcely one hour and a half after they had arrived in the woods Elizabeth saw Eleanor and Amelia talking to Sir James. The other two young men joined them and they all looked in her direction. She knew their pleasure in the exercise had long since abated, they were not as robustly dressed as she, and must all have had a considerable amount of snow fall down their necks. Every time a branch was pulled the snow flew off on whoever was unfortunate enough to be standing directly below. If she was honest, she too was ready to return, but was determined to complete her task despite the fact that she would no longer be able to arrange the decorations as she wished.

Sir James strode up to her. She could not see his expression as he kept his head lowered, making sure he didn't suffer the same fate as young Mr Bloomfield who had tumbled backwards into a snow drift when he put an unwary foot down a rabbit hole.

'Miss Baverstock, the ladies have decided they have done enough today. They are cold and wet, as are we all, and wish to return to the house to get warm and dry. I insist that you come too. Smith is quite capable of completing the collection, he tells me he's been doing it since you were in leading strings.'

She hesitated. He was quite correct, but giving up was not in her nature. Then she recalled that this would be her very last Christmas in residence, so what did it matter *who* collected the greenery? She would not be there to do it in future years.

'Very well, I shall be glad to accompany you. Cook is making leek and vegetable soup and beef pasties for luncheon, and it seems a long time ago since I ate that half a pineapple.'

'Good girl! Here, take my arm and

I'll guide you back to the others.'

She remembered the sly pinches she'd received from Amelia during the morning to remind her that she was only with them on sufferance, and this made her refuse. 'Thank you, Sir James, but wouldn't it be more appropriate if you were to walk back with your . . . with Eleanor.'

He glanced at the waiting group and smiled ruefully. 'Perhaps, in the circumstances, it might be wiser for us not to walk together. There is one amongst us who seems determined to find fault with your behaviour. Don't let her intimidate you, my dear, you have as much right to be here — no, more right to be here — than she does.'

Buoyed up by his perspicacity she called her farewells to the hard-working men and left them to complete the filling of the cart. The contents would be transferred to the flower room where it should have been her task to sort it all out. However, as Amelia had insisted *she* was in charge she would leave everything in that person's overconfident hands. The Christmas ball was to be held on the 23rd of December, it not being seemly to have such an occasion on Christmas Eve itself. Last year the house had still been in mourning so the Hall had not been decorated; this year Elizabeth was determined to have a hand in organising the greenery. She wanted one last chance to see the house decked out in its festive finery. She would leave Amelia until teatime. By when she would surely have become bored and abandoned the task; no one could possibly object if *she* stepped in to complete the work.

David Bloomfield made no attempt to walk at her side. No doubt he had been told she was of no account by Amelia. As they approached the rear of the house she branched off and entered through the servants' door. She was greeted by Mrs Blake.

'My dear Miss Elizabeth, you resemble a snowman. I'm glad you decided to leave it to the outdoor men to finish, you overtax yourself. One of these days your strength will fail you if you don't take care.'

'Mrs Blake, I am as strong as a horse and we both know it. I admit I have lost weight, and do not sleep as well as I might, but a little outside exercise never did me any harm. My head cold has all but gone, only someone with a healthy constitution would have recovered so quickly.'

'Why don't you retire to your rooms, get yourself warm and dry and put your feet up for a bit? I shall send Tilly and Jenny along with hot water for you. A tray will come in half an hour when you're warm and dry.'

Smiling at the constant kindness of those it used to be her job to take care of, Elizabeth hurried up the back stairs and out on to the nursery floor. There was still ice on the inside of the windows at the far end that overlooked the park, and she shivered at the thought of having a strip wash in such unpleasant conditions. On pushing open the school room door, which doubled as her parlour, she stopped in surprise. Fires had been lit at both ends of the room, two baskets of logs stood ready beside each grate and four scuttles of coal stood by them. She ran into her bed chamber and found the same had been done for her there. Small wonder Mrs Blake had been eager for her to return to her apartments.

Her ablutions were a pleasure. It would have been even nicer to have sufficient water to fill a tub, but she managed by standing in a china basin and tipping the water over herself when necessary. After dressing in a warm tea-gown of damask rose twill, she used the remainder of the water to sponge the mud from the hem of her velvet gown. It would dry beautifully hanging over the back of a chair in front of one of the fires.

Her tray had arrived in her absence and not only were the expected treats upon it but also a mug of steaming chocolate and a slice of Cook's delicious plum cake. This was a feast indeed and for the first time in many months she could do justice to it. She had just pushed away her plate and was shaking the crumbs from her gown when the door of the school room flew open.

Lady Hartford stood framed in the doorway, the crimson egret feathers bobbing wildly in her turban. Her eyes were hard, her lips thin; she stared around the chamber with growing disbelief.

'As I thought. Someone shall be dismissed for this, young lady. I gave no sanction to you having one fire in here, and you now have two. I'll not be ignored in this way.' Her eyes snapped with venom. 'And where, pray, did the flowers and fruit come from?'

'The fruit and flowers came from Sir James, so you must take the matter up with him, it was none of my doing. I ordered the fires, the footmen could hardly disobey me, they have been following my bidding for many years.' This only added to her ladyship's fury. Not allowing her to start a second tirade Elizabeth continued, 'I wished to be warm for once. I shall tell you now what I had intended to keep secret. I have accepted the position of governess with a prestigious family in Yorkshire. I take up my employment immediately after Christmas. I have already booked my seat on the mail coach.'

For a moment her adversary seemed bemused by this statement, then she rallied and Elizabeth saw the same triumph in her expression as she had seen earlier in Amelia's. 'That's an excellent idea. You are not welcome here. With you gone we shall not be constantly reminded of our shortcomings.'

'Then you will dismiss no one? Allow me to have a final Christmas in comfort, one last opportunity to join in the festivities before leaving for ever.'

'Amelia told me you have insinuated yourself with Sir James and Mr

Bloomfield and his brother, that you have invited yourself to the ball. It shall be your swansong, miss, but do not think you may come down to dine with us, neither will you fraternise with the guests in future. That would be the outside of enough. Be satisfied you may remain in luxury up here and attend our gala occasion the day after tomorrow.'

Standing straight and proud Elizabeth did not flinch. 'If there is nothing else, madam, I bid you good day.'

Unused to being sent away by someone she thought too cowed and beholden to fight back, her ladyship fired her final riposte. 'I warn you, miss, that if you disobey me in this matter I shall turn away six of the oldest and most vulnerable staff. They shall leave this establishment when you do.'

The door slammed shut behind her. Elizabeth wished she'd not eaten so heartily for her stomach threatened to rebel. This was the one thing she feared the most. There were several elderly retainers who had been with the family for the whole of their working life. If they were dismissed they would surely starve. This was unthinkable. How could Grandpa have been so remiss? He had been the kindest of men, never had a cross word to say to anyone, was respected and loved by everyone throughout his vast estate. Why had he not had the foresight to provide for his staff? Indeed, the fact that his will could not be found bemused his lawyers. Goodness — legal crows had all but ransacked the office and study to find the errant document. But there was nothing she could do about it. There was no point in repining, it was up to her to protect these people until she finally departed.

Tears filled her eyes as she realised the futility of this. Half the staff would be sent packing as soon as she had gone, to be replaced by people who would not cast judgement on the new Lord and Lady Hartford, would not find them wanting. She was in no position to provide for her loyal retainers, she barely had enough to take her safely to her employment. She paced the length of the school room unable to enjoy the unaccustomed warmth, her emotions in turmoil thinking about the fate of the loyal staff who had devoted their lives to the Hartford family. It was impossible to remain here as instructed; she would creep down to the study. This room was seldom used as the present earl took no interest in running the estate, leaving all that to the manager. Elizabeth was certain Mr Bishop did a far better job left to his own devices than if someone like Lord Hartford was constantly interfering. As long as his lordship saw funds flowing into his coffers he would be satisfied.

Although the fire in the study was unlit, it was made and ready for her to push a taper into the kindling. The curtains were half drawn, the large desk and the other items of furniture undusted. She would occupy her time

71

rectifying these omissions. Grandpa had loved this room and they had spent many happy hours together in front of the fire. The library ran the entire length of the upper floor, but was not conducive to a comfortable coze, it was far too big for that. Over the years she had selected books to read and then taken them down to the study where she would curl up in an armchair and watch her grandfather work at his extraordinary desk. He had told her it came from far off India, had been crafted especially for him there and carried across the Himalayas on the backs of two donkeys. No doubt the current incumbents disliked the faded furnishings and elderly armchairs, but fortunately Lady Hartford's ruthless improvements had not yet reached this room. It would be heartbreaking to see it transformed into yet another homage to the Egyptians.

The cleaning materials she required were kept in a large cupboard down-stairs in the servants' quarters. She stopped to talk to several maids and footmen on her way who were eager to tell her that Amelia had already abandoned the flower room and retreated to the grand drawing-room where the young people were organising a pantomime to be performed on the day after Christmas. No doubt the older folk were occupied in other pursuits, she was sure they would not wish to participate in anything so active as a pantomime. With the wooden box filled with beeswax polish, dusters and damp cloths she hurried back to the study. Once inside she donned her apron. Now the fire was alight it would be a shame to waste the fuel. When the room was pristine once more she would take over where Amelia had left off.

An hour later she was satisfied everything was as it should be apart from the desk itself. This was an ornate item with many drawers and nooks and crannies, and it would take far too long to polish this today. She tucked the cleaning materials under the kneehole and, still enveloped in her apron and voluminous cap, she headed for the flower room.

The sound of voices and activity inside meant that the designated staff had not also abandoned the job — so much the better, it was an arduous task to twine holly, ivy and other evergreens into the garlands needed to drape across the overmantels in all the reception rooms.

'Miss Baverstock, thank goodness you have come to organise matters. We are sadly adrift, here and have no notion how to do things.'

Sir James was standing at the sink in his shirt sleeves vainly attempting to weave the branches together. Several other guests were in there also, none of them known to her. She hesitated in the doorway, uncertain if she should so blatantly disobey Lady Hartford's instructions. If Amelia and Eleanor, and the Bloomfield gentlemen were not with this party, perhaps she could do this and still remain undetected by the family.

'It's very kind of you all to offer to help. I'm afraid I have only been introduced to Sir James.'

'Allow me to introduce you. The remainder of the house party are involved with some kind of playacting, we are the remnants who do not enjoy such pastimes.' He proceeded to name the others and Miss Baverstock curtsied politely to each. He could not help contrasting this tall, plain girl with the two beautiful Hartford girls. However, there was something about her that wrung his heartstrings, made him want to protect her. Although she was of far stronger character than Eleanor, she had a vulnerability about her that the other girl did not.

She proceeded to organise them ruthlessly. Within half an hour the first garland was ready to be carried into the entrance hall and all the participants in the exercise were thoroughly enjoying themselves. Four young footmen had been summoned to carry the object.

'I must supervise the positioning of this, can I trust the rest of you to continue with your tasks without slacking in my absence?'

The two young ladies and the other gentlemen sang out their agreement. 'Miss Baverstock, you are a hard taskmaster, but are your servants not to have refreshments?'

'Of course, Miss Culley, but not until we have completed the decorations for the vestibule.' Her extraordinary violet eyes were sparkling with mischief. She was almost pretty when she was animated.

'I demand that we stop for afternoon tea as soon as you return. This is not negotiable, your workers shall lay down their tools if they are denied sustenance.'

'In which case, Sir James, I suggest that you ring the bell above your head and order what you require. However, I think we cannot join the others in our current dishevelment. Would you care to take tea in the study? I lit a fire earlier, it will be far warmer there than it is in here.'

He bowed and grabbed the bell strap. Unfortunately his tug was too vigorous and it came away from the ceiling, covering him in plaster. Her laughter at his predicament was worth the discomfort of having half the ceiling down his neck.

'Oh dear! How unfortunate. I do believe that now, Sir James, I cannot allow you into the study.' He could hear her laughing as she directed the footmen carrying the first of the garlands. Somehow he thought this girl didn't have cause to laugh very often.

★   ★   ★

The greenery interwoven with red and green ribbon looked stunning draped across the mantel. All that was needed to complete it were the fat yellow candles pushed in amongst it. 'George, will you hang this wreath of holly above the fireplace, and Bill climb up the stepladder and attach the bunch of mistletoe to the central chandelier.'

There were several smaller garlands to drape along the window sills, and arrangements of silver and gold painted fir cones, interspersed with ribbons, to put out on the various pieces of furniture. As she turned to go and collect the other items Sir James appeared, still liberally covered with plaster and without his jacket, carrying one of the swags and followed closely by the other guests with the remaining decorations.

'Miss Baverstock, where would you like these things placed?'

She could hardly tell him she was forbidden to fraternise with the guests or that at any moment Amelia might appear and carry tales to Lady Hartford. 'You are all so kind. The garlands are for the windowsills, the baskets of fir cones to go on the sideboards and tables.'

Amidst much hilarity her assistants did as she bid. Elizabeth flinched every time she heard a voice from the drawing-room and Sir James must have observed her nervousness for he came across and drew her to one side where they could not be overheard.

'Miss Baverstock, you must not worry about being taken to task. I can assure you that whilst I am here I shall make it my business . . . '

'Oh no, sir, you must not bother yourself on my behalf. It will just cause unpleasantness. Lady Hartford is already annoyed with you for sending up your gifts, it would not do to upset her further.'

'I have broad shoulders, my dear, please allow me to stand between you.'

For some reason she found herself pouring out all that had transpired that day and about the missing will. As she spoke, his face changed from friendly to ferocious. She wished she'd held her tongue — now she had offended him as well by her tale bearing.

'That is outrageous! You have as much right to mingle with the guests as the Hartfords. And to threaten you in that way, it's inexcusable. I insist that you dine with us tonight. I can promise you, you will not be slighted.'

Her distress over her interview with her ladyship evaporated beneath his concern. 'I prefer to dine in my own chambers, thank you, Sir James. But in future I shall certainly make sure that I am around during the day to join in the festivities.' How could she have thought him rude and overbearing? He was the *kindest* man imaginable.

'You are coming to the ball, are you not? You will not hide upstairs when that is taking place.'

When he smiled at her she felt anything was possible. 'I am so looking forward to it. Do you know, I have never been to a formal dance of any sort. To attend such a grand occasion will be truly wonderful.'

'I trust that you have not been given the task of decorating the ballroom as well as the other chambers?'

'Of course not, that is a task that has

been given to Mrs Blake and Mr Foster, they are much better suited to it than I.' She stepped back to admire their work and was delighted at the charming effect she had created. 'Thank you all so much for helping me. I shall fully understand if you do not wish to continue after tea, you have done more than enough already.'

Miss Culley, a diminutive young lady with russet curls and an impish smile, impulsively threw her arms around her. 'Miss Baverstock, I declare I've never had so much fun in all my life as I've had this afternoon. I, for one, shall continue until the whole house looks as beautiful as this grand space.'

'Please, won't you call me Elizabeth? I believe that we are already firm friends.'

'And you must call me Sarah. Come along everyone, I can smell tea and hot scones somewhere down this passage-way.'

Sir James stepped up and offered his arm. 'Allow me to escort you to the study, Miss Baverstock.' He grinned down at her. 'Or rather, would you escort me, as I have no notion where to find the study.'

He did not see Amelia standing in the doorway watching him smiling down at Elizabeth. If he had he might have been on his guard and been able to prevent what later took place.

5

Cook had excelled herself. Not only was there tea *and* coffee, but also a substantial plate of warm scones and a bowl of thick cream and strawberry conserve to go with them. Elizabeth was pleased her new friends had been treated to one of Cook's specialities. Two smiling parlour maids were there to serve them.

Soon they were all sitting around, Mr Miller and Mr Crew perched on the window seats and Sarah and Mrs Miller in the battered armchairs, whilst she and Sir James sat in splendid isolation at the huge desk. For a considerable time one could only hear the sound of contented munching.

'Absolutely delicious, Miss Baverstock,' Mr Miller said wiping his sticky fingers on a clean linen napkin. 'Normally I'm not one for sweet things, as my dear wife will agree. However, if these scrumptious morsels appear again I shall certainly be first in line.'

Judging by the size of his waist Mr Miller was not being strictly truthful. Smiling, Elizabeth drained her teacup. 'I'm so glad I took the time to clean this room earlier, otherwise there would have been dust to add to your white coating, Sir James.' She ran her finger over the carved surface of the desk and shook her head. 'However, I did not have time to polish this monstrosity.'

'Ah! I had wondered why I was sharing foot space with a box of cleaning materials.' Without warning he vanished under the desk to reappear with the wooden box. 'Come along, ladies and gentlemen, our domestic chores are not complete. We must polish this desk before we return to the flower room.'

Elizabeth leapt to her feet in consternation. This would not do! It was one thing for her to be engaged in servant's duties but quite another for

the guests. Arranging Christmas greenery was quite acceptable, polishing a
desk was not. 'Please, there is no need.
No one uses this room, indeed I don't
think I've been in here more than a
couple of times since . . . since my
grandfather passed over.'

Sir James had other ideas. He was
rather a highhanded gentleman with a
tendency to take command quite
unnecessarily. 'If you have completed
your repast, I suggest that Miss Culley
remains behind with Miss Baverstock
and myself to complete the task. The
rest of you have a dozen more garlands
to make.'

Sarah smiled and pointed to the
mistletoe. 'I do hope you intend to put
bunches of *that* in the ballroom as well
as the hall?'

'I had not thought of it. The
decoration of that chamber is being
completed by the staff alone. However,
Sarah, I'm sure if you tie a bunch with
that red ribbon and take it along it will
be put up for you.'

The others trooped out leaving her alone with Sarah and Sir James. It was decidedly strange that he showed no inclination to join Eleanor in the drawing-room. If he was intending to make her an offer surely he should be at her side? She handed out a soft cloth to each of them and then placed the polish where they could all dip in.

'This is a horrible thing to polish, it has so many bumps and lumps and curly bits. I think that's why none of the staff come in here, they know it will take them hours to complete *this* task.'

They worked happily whilst chatting about the forthcoming ball. Sarah informed them that the pantomime that was to be presented by a small group of guests, the ensemble led by Amelia and her sister as the female leads and the two Bloomfield gentlemen as the heroes. She was surprised that Eleanor was prepared to perform in public, she was normally so shy. However it was a good sign. Sir James would much prefer a wife who was not timid. Good grief!

She scarcely knew the gentleman and here she was thinking she knew what sort of woman he would wish to marry.

They were so engrossed in their polishing none of them heard the door open but all three heads jerked around in shock at Lady Hartford's screech.

'Sir James, Miss Culley, I cannot believe my eyes. I am so mortified to find to my guests doing such a task. I shall never live down the shame. Elizabeth, how could you? Go at once to your chamber. Lord Hartford is waiting to speak to you.'

Elizabeth dropped the polishing rag as if it burnt her fingers. Without looking to see how her disgrace was viewed by the others she ran from the room. She prayed that his lordship was in fact not upstairs, that this was merely a ploy to remove her from circulation. As she fled through the house she kept her eyes lowered not wishing to see the disgust in the eyes of those guests that she passed. She was breathless when she arrived at the schoolroom, where a pair of stony faced footmen were waiting by the door. These were recently employed, their loyalty firmly with the present Lord Hartford. Determined not to seem at all perturbed by being sent to her room like a recalcitrant child, she stared at them frostily and stalked past. To her horror the room was not empty as she had hoped.

'Well, miss, this is a fine way to repay my generosity, I must say. When her ladyship informed me that firstly you had disobeyed her direct instructions and then had the temerity to get my daughter's intended involved in your menial work, I thought she was exaggerating.' He puffed his cheeks, seeming to swell before her like a barnyard fowl. He certainly dressed as gaudily as a cockerel, and with his rubicund complexion and bald pate he was not a man who impressed one with his elegance and gentility. Keeping this image in her mind made it easier for her to remain calm instead of showing how frightened she really was.

'Amelia abandoned the decorations, my lord. I had no option but to go down and finish the job myself. I did not invite any of your guests to join me, they were already in the flower room when I arrived.'

'Do not attempt to excuse yourself, my girl, do not try and place the blame on Amelia. I suppose that Sir James offered to polish the furniture as well? No doubt he occupies his leisure hours in such pastimes at Brackenfield.'

It was pointless arguing with him. She must accept whatever punishment he offered. She held his gaze, and was pleased to see him flush. 'I beg your pardon, my lord, if doing my duty has somehow offended you.'

His fists clenched and for an awful moment she thought he was going to strike her. He stepped back, shaking his head. 'As my dear wife tells me you are leaving very soon I shall not give you the beating you deserve. However, you will remain locked in your chambers

89

until the time comes for your departure.' He looked around the room, taking in the flowers and fruit, the brightly burning fires and abundance of fuel. 'There will be no more logs or coal sent up, and as you have more than enough to eat already, there shall be bread and water in future.' He sneered triumphantly as he reached the door. 'If you set foot from this chamber, six of the oldest servants will be sent packing, without reference or payment. Also if you have any further contact with *any* of the guests, expect a further six to be tramping through the snow.'

Somehow she remained resolute, continuing to stare at him disdainfully, but no sooner had the door closed behind him than the cruelty of his decision overwhelmed her. Perhaps he was hoping she would pack her bags and run away today rather than be treated like a prisoner in an institution. He would not get that satisfaction. She would leave on the appointed day with head held high.

James was shocked to the core by Lady Hartford's outburst. In that moment he came to a momentous decision — he could not possibly affiliate himself to this family. To have this appalling, vulgar woman as his mother-in-law would be quite impossible. It was as if a weight lifted from his shoulders. He realised now that he felt no more than a mild affection for Eleanor, not nearly enough on which to base a lifelong union.

'Lady Hartford, Miss Culley and I insisted that we helped Miss Baverstock. If someone of her impeccable pedigree does not turn her back on domestic chores, then who are we to cavil?' He fully intended to explain in words of one syllable how far she fell beyond the pale by her behaviour when he recalled that she had said Lord Hartford was waiting to speak to Elizabeth.

He threw down his cloth and stepped around the objectionable harridan and bolted for the stairs. If that man raised a finger to Elizabeth he would take a horsewhip to him. He arrived on the nursery floor as his lordship stepped out. The portly man recoiled and the colour drained from his face.

'Sir James . . . I cannot imagine what brings you up here.'

'Can you not, my lord? Remain where you are, I wish to speak to Miss Baverstock in your presence.'

'If you insist, I shall not stand in your way.'

James rapped on the door and heard light footsteps approaching. The door was opened a fraction and a face he scarcely recognized appeared in the gap. What had he done to this girl? Her beautiful eyes were tear-filled and her face chalk-white. 'My dear, I gave you my word I would protect you from harm. You must tell me at once if this . . . this person has hurt you.'

She shook her head vigorously. 'No, his lordship has done nothing unto-ward. I should not have involved you in my tasks, I beg your pardon for doing so. I shall be remaining in my chambers until after the Christmas festivities. Please do not contact me again under any circumstances.'

The door snapped shut and she was gone. James turned, prepared to shake the truth out of his lordship, but he was alone on the landing. Whilst his attention had been elsewhere the coward had sloped off taking his two bodyguards with him. There was nothing he could do up here. Elizabeth had made her feelings plain. Hartford must have some hold over her and James would do nothing further to aggravate the situation. However, there was one thing he could do — he could search that extraordinary desk and look for secret hiding places. There was a remote possibility that the missing will would prove to be hidden in there. Although, as he no longer intended to offer for Eleanor he should pack his bags and ride away. James rested his hand on the door. He couldn't leave until he was sure Elizabeth was safe. His eyes widened. Heavens above! It could not be — surely he was not developing feelings for this unfortunate young lady? James was tempted to insist that she open the door. He wanted to see her again, remove that hideous cap and apron and see her as she really was. No, better not, not now. If he could discover the missing document he was certain it would prove that she was not the penniless dependent everyone thought. James took the stairs two at a time. The sooner he started his search, the better.

* * *

Elizabeth decided it would make more sense to keep just her bedchamber warm. With luck, there would be enough fuel for the fire in there to last until she left. Discarding her cap and apron she busied herself transferring the log baskets and coal scuttles. This task completed she carried in the flowers and fruit basket. It was fortunate she had filled herself up with scones and jam, she would not feel hungry until tomorrow. She dragged an armchair and table through and then removed the rag rug that covered the centre of the room. Keeping active gave her less time to think, to contemplate her miserable future. Two hours later her bedchamber was transformed; all her books, writing materials and watercolour equipment were safely installed on shelves. The flowers were standing proudly on the small octagonal table by the window and the fruit stored in her dressing room which was far cooler than the chamber. She would keep herself occupied painting the view from the window and filling in her journal. Then she had several novels to read and her needlepoint to finish. The time would soon fly by, before she knew it Christmas would be over and she could start her new life.

By suppertime, when not even bread and water had been brought to her, her optimism was fading. Without water to drink she would not survive her incarceration. There were several oranges in the basket but these would not provide her with the liquid she required. Deciding time would go quicker if she was asleep she readied herself for bed. Her nightgown was warming nicely by the fire, she had only to remove her undergarments and slip it on and she would be done. Quite unexpectedly her dressing room door opened and Mrs Blake trooped in with three maids.

'I'm so sorry we could not come earlier, miss, we had to wait until the mistress and master were safely retired. We have a tray for you, but you must keep some of it for tomorrow as I fear it will not be until this time again that we can come up to you.'

The delicious aroma of cook's leek and potato soup wafted over from the tureen. Her stomach gurgled loudly and her visitors laughed. Sally set a chair at the table and dished up a bowl of soup. 'Here you are, Miss Baverstock, there's fresh bread and butter to go with it. Then you have game pie and redcurrant jelly and to follow a slice of apple pie and cream.'

Not wishing to be left out, Mary chimed in. 'We have brought you a large jug of lemonade, hot water and cold, and to drink now, a pot of coffee.'

'Thank you — but you have risked your positions to bring me this. I could not bear it if you were to be dismissed because of me. I see you have plum cake, cheese and pickles on the other tray. With the fruit I already have I shall manage for a day or two. You must not come again tomorrow, it's far too risky.'

For the first time Ann, who was the household seamstress, spoke up. 'Food is not the only reason we have come, Miss Baverstock. I have brought my pins and measuring tape. We are going to make you a ball gown.'

Elizabeth felt her throat thicken. How could she tell them she did not dare to go to the ball, even if she they managed to make her something suitable? 'How kind of you. Do you intend to alter something that I already own? I fear there's nothing suitable in my closet for such a grand occasion.

Like a conjuror Ann reached behind her and a cascade of gold tipped over the rag rug. Elizabeth fell to her knees burying her hands in the silken material. It was soft and shimmering. When she held it to the candlelight it sparkled as if lit up by tiny gemstones. 'This is so beautiful. Where did you find it?'

The four of them exchanged conspiratorial glances, but it was Mrs Blake who answered. 'Never you mind about where it came from, my love, it's yours by right and we're going to sew you the most beautiful dress anyone has ever seen.'

Sally held a swathe of the material up to Elizabeth's face. 'See, the colour's perfect with your pale gold hair. I shall make ribbons from the scraps and thread these through your hair. Mary is an expert at making roses, we thought to sew them in a swirl around the skirt.'

'Just a moment! I'd quite forgotten but I have something that belonged to my mama.' She dashed into the dressing room and rummaged through her sewing box. 'There, I have them.' Triumphantly she ran back and tipped the small cloth bag out on to the gossamer material. A fountain of little golden beads tumbled down.

'Oh my! These will be perfect, miss, I shall decorate the neckline and the sleeves with them,' Ann said happily.

'All we need now to complete the outfit are gloves and evening slippers. Do you have anything suitable in your closet, Miss Baverstock?'

Sadly Elizabeth shook her head. 'I haven't. I never dine formally so I have no gloves apart from those I wear outside. My only pair of slippers are black leather, but I shall wear them if I have to.'

Mrs Blake helped Ann fold up the

silk whilst Mary and Sally replaced the beads in the bag. Suddenly Elizabeth's courage returned. She *would* go to the ball. Her lack of gloves and footwear would not matter if she was wearing a gown made of this fabulous material. 'You have still not taken my measurements, Ann, nor told me what the pattern shall be.'

'I thought to use one of your gowns as a guide. If you would care to slip one on I will pin it so that it fits you exactly.'

When they eventually departed life did not seem so drear. She still had friends who cared for her, had sufficient nourishment to see her through tomorrow. And then the next day it would be the Christmas ball. It did not seem possible that the four of them could sew her gown in so short a time. They would have to sit up all night, for they certainly would not have any spare time during their working day. If only she could do something for them in return, make their lives easier in some way —

but she was as dependent as they were. She fell to her knees beside the bed and sent up a fervent plea to the Almighty that he would provide an answer to her prayer.

6

James spent some time examining the desk but could find no hidden compartment. Disappointed, he returned to his chambers to change for dinner. It had not occurred to him that the Hartfords would no longer view him as a welcome guest because of his support for Miss Baverstock. Neither Eleanor nor her sister greeted him with their customary smiles. They curtsied vaguely in his direction and immediately resumed their conversation with Ned Bloomfield and his younger brother. So be it. It was fortunate that he had changed his mind or her coldness might have disconcerted him. Occasionally during the long, tedious meal she glanced in his direction apologetically. Perhaps it was not her fault, perhaps she was merely following the instructions of her parents. He was seated next to Miss Culley on his right and her elderly aunt on his left. He did his best to entertain them both, but Miss Culley senior was as deaf as a post and her niece more interested in Lord Bloomfield who was her other dinner partner. Bloomfield had been left a widower two years ago. Fortunately his children were already old enough to manage without the guidance of their mother. Was this the way the wind blew? It certainly explained why this lively young lady had come to spend Christmas at Hartford Hall.

When the ladies withdrew and left the gentlemen to their port Bloomfield moved up a chair in order to speak privately to him. 'What's this Hartford's saying about you, old fellow? Fraternising with the staff?'

James felt a wave of anger. 'If you are referring to Miss Baverstock, the previous Earl of Hartford was her grandfather. She is better bred than the current occupiers of her ancestral home.'

'My word, my boy — is that the right of it? From what the bounder said one would have thought she was little better than a servant. Disgraceful; she ought to be dining with us.'

'I entirely agree, Bloomfield. However, for some reason she wishes to remain in her chambers. I have no notion why this is, but I intend to find out one way or another.'

He caught the eye of Ned Bloomfield and the young man nodded towards the door. He obviously wished to speak with James. Ignoring his host, James smiled at his friend, and stood up. Immediately Lord Bloomfield joined him, as did his younger son and, leaving the remaining dozen gentlemen at the table, the four of them strolled out.

'I say, Sir James, I don't like it above half you know. A poor show indeed, sending Miss Baverstock away from us. Lady Eleanor is most concerned for her welfare. Do you think we should go up and see how she does?'

James found himself warming to this

young man. His enquiry was genuine, his expression open and honest. 'I have spoken to Miss Baverstock. It would appear she wishes to remain apart from us for the present. I'm glad you and Lady Eleanor have struck up a friendship. I wish to assure you that my interest in that direction is at an end.'

'I say, that's capital news. I'd not come here looking to fall into parson's mousetrap, I'm but three and twenty, fully expect to sew my wild oats a while longer.' He grinned and tugged at his cravat. 'However, I think Lady Eleanor would be better with me and not here. It's not a happy household. I ain't one for complaining, Sir James, but I can't take to Lady Amelia or her mater and pater.'

'I'm delighted to hear you say so, young man. Get her away from the pernicious influence of her sister and parents as soon as possible, she is easily led and would become like them in time.'

Ned shook James's hand as if

drawing water from a pump. 'I shall speak to my father directly. If I have his approval I shall dip my toe in the water straightaway.'

James looked around to see if Lord Bloomfield was still in the vicinity but he had vanished into the drawing-room to join the ladies. He wandered into the entrance hall to admire the decorations. With the candles flickering amongst the leaves it looked enchanting. He was standing in the shadows when he heard voices approaching. Should he reveal himself or remain hidden where he was? He tensed. It was young Bloomfield and Eleanor. His lips curved as he saw him guide her until she was standing directly beneath the bunch of mistletoe. They were talking so softly he could not hear their words from where he was positioned, but he saw her glance upwards and laugh. Then Ned tenderly encircled her waist and drew her closer and their lips met in a passionate kiss.

Enough was enough, he could not lurk in the darkness, he must announce himself. He coughed and the two of them sprung apart and stared guiltily in his direction. She gathered up her skirts and hurried back into the drawing-room. The young man recovered his composure and bowed.

'Am I to congratulate you, sir?'

'I say, just a bit of fun, nothing like that. I ain't spoke to my father yet, he might not approve.'

James stared at him and he looked away uncomfortably. This would not do. He might not wish to marry his girl himself but he could not stand by and allow Bloomfield to play fast and loose with her good name.

'Are you sure she sees a kiss in the same way? Lady Eleanor is an innocent, she will believe that your intentions are serious. Whatever your father says on the matter, by kissing her in so public a place you must offer for her or her reputation will be irredeemably damaged.' He frowned and the young man shifted from foot to foot. 'I believe scarcely twenty minutes ago you declared your intention of courting Lady Eleanor. Why should you hold back now?'

'I'm not certain she is the one for me. It's what she was saying just now that's put me off.'

James felt an urge to floor the man. He was as fickle as the worst flirt, he had no right to take the girl under the mistletoe if his intentions were no longer honourable. 'In which case, sir, your behaviour was despicable. I shall not speak of what I saw. Make certain you hold your tongue or you will answer to me.'

'Don't you want to know what it was? It concerns Miss Baverstock.'

'Well, tell me, Bloomfield.'

'She told me that Miss Baverstock is to leave next week to become a governess, and Lady Eleanor was pleased about it. She believes this to be quite acceptable but my blood boiled, I can tell you. I've a good mind to marry Miss Baverstock myself to keep her safe.'

The young man was a veritable nincompoop. James's anger turned to amusement and he clapped the boy on the back. 'Leave Miss Baverstock's welfare to me. I suggest that you return to the drawing room and do not bring any more young ladies out here. Is that quite clear?'

'Absolutely. I would not have brought Lady Eleanor out here but I wished to have her talk of other things and could think of nothing else to silence her.'

James strode back to the study. If he had met his host he doubted he could have restrained himself from punching his lordship on the nose. At least he now understood why Elizabeth — he could not continue to think of her as Miss Baverstock — why Elizabeth believed she would no longer be welcome downstairs. A governess did not socialise with the family and their guests unless there was a need to make up the numbers at table. He would write her a note, tell her . . . what could he tell her? That he wished to take care of her, that he wished to make her his wife? To marry out of pity was not a good way to start a relationship, there must at least be desire and strong affection between a couple for the union to be successful.

James slumped in despair behind the desk. He could not in all conscience do more than offer to assist her in finding a better place to live. He was still in touch with several of his late father's friends, surely one of them must have daughters of a similar age who would be willing to sponsor her? He had deep pockets, he could give Elizabeth a substantial dowry and sufficient funds to take her place in the *ton*. Once she was officially out he could get to know her better and make it his business to squire her about. He admired her intellect, her courage, her kindness and her loving heart — but she did not make his heart skip a beat. He was merely interested in her welfare, and sadly felt nothing stronger. However, it was highly unlikely she would accept

110

monetary help from him.

Drifting back into the throng he could not help but notice Miss Sarah Culley playing a lively game of piquet with Lord Bloomfield. He watched them exchange glances and smiled inwardly. He had got things wrong. Bloomfield had come to Hartford Hall not to promote the interests of his eldest son, but to spend time with Miss Culley. It was an October-May relationship, but the couple were ideally suited. She had been in society for several seasons, had received countless offers but never accepted. She was quite old enough to know her own mind. At the least there would be one couple glad there were bunches of mistletoe included in the Christmas decorations.

★　★　★

Elizabeth all but skipped out of bed on the morning of the ball. She had put jugs of water to warm by the fire and this morning she was going to wash her hair. It would take most of the day to dry, so the sooner she got it done the better. She piled logs and coal on the fire and sat on a pile of cushions with her hair floating damply around her while she toasted several slices of bread in front of the flames. It was the first time since Grandpa had died that she felt happy. She would not worry about the future, today she would think only of attending the ball. Once she was amongst the guests it would be impossible for even Lord Hartford to remove her.

She wished it had been a masked occasion then she could have remained anonymous and run away at midnight just like Cinderella in the fairy story. She giggled at her comparison. She certainly had the equivalent of a wicked stepmother and two wicked stepsisters. No, that was being unfair to Eleanor, who was weak rather than unkind. And she had no doubt who her Prince Charming was: it was Sir James. Her heart raced and she sank back into the cushions with a sigh. He had all the necessary attributes, was tall dark and handsome, courageous and strong. Had he not sworn to protect her from harm just like a prince from a story book? Elizabeth laughed out loud at her nonsense. She might think of him in romantic terms but he had never looked at her with more than kindness in his eyes. He was a good man, but he did not love her. Love? Where had that notion come from? She had known him such a short while and they'd spend much of that at loggerheads, how could she fancy herself in love with him? His image filled her head and angrily she pushed it away. It would not do to harbour such thoughts, it was her imagination playing tricks with her. He was an attractive man, that was all, she must not let herself feel anything stronger. In a few days time she would be leaving to become a governess and no man of his standing would consider her a suitable wife then. But just for tonight she would imagine she was the girl from the fairytale and that her story *would* have a happy ending like Cinderella's.

By mid-afternoon Eliabeth's hair was dry and she decided to creep up into the attics to search for something suitable to wear on her feet. She was almost certain there had been several trunks of garments that had been left behind when her mother had married her dashing young captain. She had no memory of either of her parents. Her father had died before she was born, and her mother had returned to live at Hartford Hall, where she had succumbed to the sweating sickness soon after they had arrived. But Grandpa had more than made up for her lack of parents. Elizabeth's eyes filled. She wished he was here to see her dance at her first ball. Good grief! It would also be the first time the ballroom had been used. She couldn't remember the last time she'd been in there, but from what she could recall it ran the full width of the house, which made it more than sixty feet long. There was a series of French doors that opened on to a terrace overlooking the ornamental lake. Would any of the couples go outside to spend a few stolen moments together? There had been no further fall of snow, but what had fallen was still on the ground. Not only would it be cold it might also be treacherous underfoot.

Taking a candlestick she slipped out through the dressing room door, normally used by the servants, and fingered her way along the narrow passageway until she found the stairs that led to the attics. Some watery sunlight filtered in through the dirty windowpanes; this, with her candle, should be sufficient to find what she was searching for. She paused to view the heavy oak furniture that had once graced Grandpa's apartment, and which had been banished to the attics within days of his demise. She'd not had the heart to come up and look at it at the time. When she'd discovered a pair of suitable evening slippers perhaps she would spend an hour two examining the contents of his discarded bureau and drawers.

What Elizabeth wanted was in a further room. She threaded her way around the miscellany of broken furniture, unwanted toys and other bric-a-brac to arrive considerably more dishevelled than she had been when she set out. Thank goodness she'd had the forethought to push her clean hair into one of the hideous caps. It would be the very last time she would wear one of these.

The trunks were where she'd expected. Standing her candle stick on a convenient shelf she dropped to her knees to open the first of them. This was full of bales of beautiful material, a kaleidoscope of colours that even the gloom of the attics could not smother. There were Indian muslins, Chinese silks and the finest Egyptian cottons — so *this* was where the gorgeous material from which her ball gown was being made had come.

Hastily Elizabeth re-fastened the box.

She didn't want the Hartfords to find it. It belonged to her, morally if not legally. She moved on to the second trunk and in here were beautiful, but outmoded, gowns. They were in bright colours, had daringly low-cut necklines and were drawn in tightly at the waist. Seeing these garments made her understand a little more about her long dead mother. She held one up in front of her. It would fit perfectly. Why hadn't Grandpa told her she was the same build as her mama? She rummaged through but found no footwear. These must be in the last trunk. She flung the lid back delighted to see it full of cloth bags. She knew these would contain shoes, as they were always stored this way.

A short while later Elizabeth had what she wanted: a pair of the most enchanting high-heeled evening slippers. They were studded with small golden stones which glittered when she held them to the light. She knew they would fit her, she was her mother's daughter in every physical respect. Again she locked the trunk and dropped all three keys into the shoe bag. One day she would come back and claim these boxes, but until then the contents would be safe.

Elizabeth had tarried a while examining her grandpa's effects so that it was now full dark outside. She decided to bring with her a handsome leather writing case, ideal to take with her when she left. Several times she barked her shins on protruding objects as she was unable to see them in the almost dark. It was with considerable relief that she escaped from the attics and arrived back to her own bed chamber. The ball did not start until nine o'clock, but there was to be a celebration dinner served for those guests that were in residence. Cook had been rushed off her feet these past two weeks with the preparations and a dozen or more extra staff had been taken on to help her in the kitchens. There would be a delicious supper laid out on tables in an ante-room, and champagne would be served throughout the event. Elizabeth had only tasted this the once and had not liked it. She hoped there would be lemonade or orgeat for those that didn't drink alcohol.

Elizabeth still had four hours before she had to be downstairs. When would Ann return with the dress? What if it wasn't finished in time? Elizabeth decided she would go to the ball whatever happened. Snatching up a candlestick she returned to the attics and selected the gown that had been made to go with the evening slippers. It had small capped sleeves edged with the same golden jewels, a neckline as daring as the other gowns and a skirt made up of looped layers of shimmering, diaphanous sarcenet. The underskirt was gold silk. Even if her new gown arrived in time she would wear this one. It must be more than forty years old, but was still as fresh and uncreased as if it had been placed in the trunk only yesterday. Back in the safety of her room she held it against her chest and spun around the room loving the way it swirled out in a golden rainbow. Then she considered how hurtful it would be if she rejected the hard work and loving attention of her friends. The dress must be hidden in her closet. Maybe one day she would have the opportunity to wear it.

7

When seven o'clock came and went
Elizabeth decided to start her preparations. She had already laid out two sets
of undergarments, one best suited to
the old-fashioned gown, the other for
the one with a high waist if it was ready
in time. The same silk stockings and
shoes would do for both. She had no
need to take a reticule, but she would
carry the lovely ivory fan she'd
discovered amongst the shoe bags. She
flicked it open to admire the ladies
painted on it. They all had white
powdered wigs and were wearing gowns
similar to the one she had hanging in
her closet. She had no glass in her bed
chamber. It was going to be difficult
arranging her hair without being able to
see her reflection.

Even in her eyrie at the top of the
house she could hear the sound of

merriment downstairs. By now all the guests would be halfway through their dinner and for once she wished she could be there to see the formal dining room being used as it should be. It was nonsense for the family to sit around the massive table every night and only be able to converse by shouting down the room. To be marooned in a sea of white damask and glittering silver cutlery this way was the height of folly in her opinion. She and Grandpa had never eaten in there, they'd always dined in the smaller room that over-looked the park. Thinking of him made her sad, but she knew he would not wish her to be still grieving after so long. She paced restlessly until eventually her fairy godmothers arrived, Mary in the lead, her face split by the broadest smile.

'Mrs Blake sends her apologies, miss, but she can't get away at the moment. It's pandemonium in the kitchen, what with a dinner with ever so many removes and the supper for later to deal with.'

'If none of you had been able to come, I should not have blamed you in the slightest. But I am so thrilled you're here, I was dreading having to arrange my hair for myself.'

'Well, you sit down and Sally and I will do it for you. The dress is not to be peeped at, miss, not until you're ready to leave.'

After what seemed like an age the girls declared themselves satisfied with the result. 'You look like a princess, Miss Baverstock. There will be no one to match you at the ball, that's for sure.'

'Thank you, Sally, but I hope that you're exaggerating. I have no wish to be the centre of attention in that way, I wish to be able to dance just once, to know what it's like to be held in the arms of a gentleman and whirled around the floor.'

She was led to the centre of the room and told to close her eyes. She felt the slither of the silk against her bare skin and shivered in excited anticipation. The three of them fiddled and fussed and then stepped back. A strange silence hung in the air. For an awful moment she thought the dress might be a disaster. Then she opened eyes and saw all three staring as if they did not recognize her.

'Miss Baverstock, I had no idea you were so . . . could look so beautiful.' Mary brushed tears from her cheeks and reached out to touch Elizabeth's hair. 'It looks like the palest gold. I've never seen the like.'

The sound of carriages pulling up in the turning circle reminded them all that it was time for Elizabeth to go. Impulsively she ran forward and kissed each in turn. 'I cannot thank you enough. I shall never forget tonight. I do indeed feel like a fairy princess with my hair arranged this way and such a beautiful ball gown. Do not attempt to come back tonight, I shall tell you all about it in the morning.'

Sally laughed. 'We shall know long before then, miss, all the old staff know what's happening. You cannot believe how many have helped to sew this gown for you. You enjoy yourself, show *them* what a real lady looks like.'

Elizabeth was tempted to creep down the back stairs and slip in to the ballroom unnoticed. However, tonight she would walk down the grand staircase as was her birthright. Her life here was all but over, what better way to end it than in a gesture of defiance?

⋆   ⋆   ⋆

Dinner had been enjoyable, the food splendid, and tonight he had been seated next to Sarah and Louise Bloomfield. He had been admirably entertained by the two young ladies, but the occasion seemed sadly flat. Surely it could not be because Miss Baverstock was not to attend?

No one dallied over port this evening. Lord and Lady Hartford and their daughters were needed in the grand hall to greet the rest of the guests who were attending the Christmas ball. He spent some time talking to Lord Bloomfield and Miss Culley and then thought he might as well drift into the hall and watch the world go by. He might see someone he was acquainted with which would raise his spirits a little.

The massive tree trunk was burning merrily, apple logs pushed in around it to make the air sweet smelling. With the candles glowing amongst the holly, ivy and fir, it was an enchanted scene. James smiled wryly. All it needed was a fairytale princess and a handsome Prince Charming to make the picture complete. The massive area was brimming with folk. Outer garments had been discarded in two ante-rooms set by for that purpose and the guests were now enjoying the festive atmosphere. Bewigged and liveried footmen glided in and out of the crowd with trays of chilled champagne. James took one as it passed and sipped thoughtfully. He had little to celebrate this Christmas. He had thought to start the

New Year with a bride, to bring laughter and happiness back to his empty home. He stared morosely into the flames, then became aware that the hall had fallen silent. James spun and his heart almost stopped. A vision of loveliness was floating down the stairs, her glorious pale golden hair threaded through with golden ribbons. Her gown floated around her like a spun gold. He clutched the mantelshelf for support and his glass dropped from his fingers to bounce into the grate unnoticed.

He knew who it was. There could only be one woman here tonight with stunning violet eyes. How could he ever have thought her plain? Her beauty was there, it was the hideous garments she was obliged to wear that had bemused him. His hands were clammy, his pulse frantic. Elizabeth was the woman of his dreams. A murmur of appreciation rippled around the people gathered there, but it was he that stepped forward and offered her his hand.

* * *

Halfway down Elizabeth hesitated, not to draw attention to herself but because she'd seen Sir James, magnificent in black, staring into the fire. He had adopted the modern fashion of pantaloons and black slippers, his cravat fell in a snowy waterfall, but it was his waistcoat and single diamond fob that held her attention. His waistcoat was gold silk and his fob in the shape of a rose. Her breath caught in her throat. It was as if fate had somehow conspired to link them tonight. Her hand came up to touch the exquisitely made golden roses that edged her neckline and her eyes shone with excitement. This evening would he be her Prince Charming?

Elizabeth was so engrossed in her fantasy that she was initally unaware of the interest she was creating amongst the newly arrived guests. Those that had begun to walk through the grand drawing room to the ballroom came

128

back to stare at her as well. Her feet became glued to the step, she could go neither up nor down, she was making a complete cake of herself. Then he turned and his eyes widened, she saw his glass drop from his slack fingers.

James strode towards her, his eyes holding her by their passion. He ran up to meet her and offered her his hand. She placed her own in his and something decidedly peculiar fizzled up her arm and around her already overheated body.

'My dear, you look amazing, beautiful, enchanting . . . that ensemble is perfection on you.' His strong, lean fingers closed over hers and drew her close beside him. She was incapable of speech, her tongue appeared to have stuck itself to the roof of her mouth. 'I understand now why the Hartfords wished to keep your glorious hair hidden under a cap. Its beauty is incomparable.'

'Sir James, we must go down, we are creating a spectacle standing here like this. Someone will have run to tell Lady Hartford and she will spoil everything.'

His laughter rang out across the hall. 'Not tonight, my love. Tonight we are invincible.'

The gathered guests stood aside as they approached smiling and nodding and offering encouragement. Most of them were known to Elizabeth but she had not seen them for a long time, as she had been forbidden to pay visits in the neighbourhood. She was not as alone as she had thought; she had the most attractive man in England at her side and was surrounded by old friends of the family who would have been puzzled as to why she had vanished from local society so long.

The orchestra was tuning up ready for the opening waltz. He stepped away to speak urgently to footmen before returning to her side.

'No, Sir James, we must not. It should be Amelia who leads the dancers out.'

James tightened his hold and again she felt that strange frisson at his touch.

'You are the true Hartford here, it's high time you were restored to your proper place in the community.'

Elizabeth was propelled forward into the vast empty space. She did not imagine the shocked gasps and felt a wave of disapproval wash over her. Then the first notes of the waltz filled the ballroom and she forgot everything; her worries about the future, about the fate of her loyal retainers, about the fact that she was hopelessly in love with the man who was staring at her in a most compelling way. Tonight she *was* Cinderella, the world was at her feet and she had until midnight to pretend she was meant to be here.

James's hand rested in the small of her back, its heat burning through the thin material of her gown. She placed her hand in his and he swept her away. As they swirled from one end of the ballroom to the other she felt as if her feet were inches from the floor. His eyes blazed down at her. She was mesmerised. The required space between their bodies slowly vanished as his arms tightened and she was drawn closer and closer. She wished the dance could go on for ever, she was incandescent with joy. Vaguely she was aware that other couples had joined them on the polished parquet floor and occasionally she caught a glimpse of Amelia or Eleanor dancing. She knew without being told which of these lovely young women in silver and white spangled gauze was which. Eleanor smiled happily at her as she passed whilst Amelia gave her dagger glances.

'My dear, the waltz is over. I believe a quadrille is to come next, shall we join a set or do you wish to . . .'

'If we dance together now, I shall have nothing more to look forward to for the rest of the evening. I shall take to the floor with no one else.'

James had not released her from his embrace when the music had stopped. He smiled in such a way that if he had not been supporting her she might have swooned at his feet. 'Tonight we shall dance every dance together, defy convention. I care not what anyone says.'

Should she point out to him that her reputation would be in tatters? To appear on the dance floor with the same partner more than twice was tantamount to announcing their intention to marry. But she was going to drop out of his circle in a few days and would probably never see him again. It no longer mattered what anyone thought. 'Sir James, I cannot promise to do that.' His smile slipped at her words and she was warmed by his desire to remain at her side no matter what. 'I fear I shall be too fatigued to stand up every time. Should you mind very much if we missed one or two in order for me to catch my breath?'

'You were funning me . . . as long as you spend every second at my side I care not whether we are dancing or sitting out.'

As the quartet struck up a lively jig Elizabeth had no time to consider anything apart from her steps. It was one thing dancing at an informal family affair with only half a dozen couples, quite another to be surrounded by people all much better versed than she in the intricacies of the dance. By the time they promenaded for the second time she was certain she would make no further errors and could relax and enjoy herself.

'There, sweetheart, you have it pat, now will you stop clutching my hand as if you were drowning and speak to me.'

This was not the first time he'd larded his remarks with endearments. It was all very well pretending to be Cinderella but each time he spoke lovingly her heart responded. He was taking their play-acting too far. 'Sir James, kindly desist from using phrases that are quite unacceptable between strangers. Do you have any conception of what people will think if they overhear you?'

He didn't answer, merely smiled, and for the rest of the set they laughed and talked of commonplaces like everyone else. When the final strains were played, he bowed and she sank into a deep curtsy. He raised her hand and slipped her arm through his. 'Shall we sit the next dance out? There will be another waltz in a while, I would like to return for that.'

They strolled, with the other couples who were leaving the floor, to one side of the ballroom. Elizabeth was pleased to be able to exchange pleasantries with neighbours she'd not seen for more than two years. The Hartfords and their cronies remained grouped together muttering and sending dark looks in her direction. So far they had done nothing to upset the watching tabbies, but when she and Sir James danced together for the third time then they *would* have something to be scandalised about.

He guided her expertly through the press of people and out into the drawing-room, and then they were in the empty vestibule. When she had descended the stairs she had not really had time to take in how lovely it looked. How kind of him to bring her back to admire her handiwork.

'Look up, my love, I brought you here for this.'

Elizabeth tilted her head and saw they were standing directly under the beribboned bunch of mistletoe. Too late she saw his intention; she could not escape. James transferred one hand to the back of her head whilst the other pulled her tight against him. His lips touched hers and she was lost, sent headlong into a place where anything was possible. Her hands slid of their own volition up his jacket to bury themselves in the thick dark hair at the back of his neck. Her feet were floating; she forgot everything, decorum and etiquette, and kissed him back. It was he that came to his senses and gently put her back on the floor.

'There's something most particular I wish to ask you. I think we can be private in the study.'

Taking hands they ran like children down the passageway and into the deserted chamber. Strangely there was a fire burning, the room was warm and then she saw a bottle of champagne and two crystal flutes standing on a silver tray in the middle of the desk ready for them. (So *that* was what he had been talking to the footmen about.)

Elizabeth was unable to do more than smile, she had no words to express her joy. Before she could regain her breath she was in his arms again and this time she knew exactly what to do. Her lips parted to receive his kiss. She had not known such pleasure existed in the world, that a gentleman's attention could send her pulses racing and make her head spin with excitement. Suddenly she was being carried across the room. It was a night for new experiences and surprises.

'I wish you to sit here, my love.' His brow creased. 'Will it damage your beautiful gown to do so?'

'I care not if it does, I am quite

prepared to sit on the floor if that's what you wish me to do.'

He lowered her into one of the battered armchairs, his smile wicked. 'Perhaps we can both do so later on, sweetheart.'

Her cheeks turned scarlet. He was outrageous! But she knew she was safe in his company, that he would never take advantage of her in any way. She occupied herself with smoothing out the folds of her skirts whilst she recovered her composure. This done she straightened and waited expectantly for what she was certain would come next.

His face was serious, his beautiful blue eyes holding her captive. As he dropped to one knee he took her hands in his and raised them to his mouth, he kissed each fingertip in turn before resting them against his pounding heart.

'Miss Baverstock, Elizabeth, my darling love — will you do me the inestimable honour of agreeing to be my wife? I know we have been acquainted barely four days but when I saw you coming down the stairs tonight I realised that I loved you.'

Slowly she withdrew her hands. 'Not until then? I wonder, why was that?'

'Your true beauty was hidden under the hideous garments you were wearing, I did not see you clearly until then.'

'What we have said and done this evening is make-believe, Sir James. You do not truly love me, you have been carried away by the enchantment of it all. Fortunately for you I shall not hold you to your offer, but I wish you had not done this. I wish we could have had one more waltz before harsh reality reclaimed me.'

Before he could deny her words she was on her feet and out through the open door. He called her back, but she was through the hidden door that led to the back stairs before he emerged from the study. With her heart breaking she stumbled along the twisting corridors, in the pitch darkness, eventually finding her bed chamber after more than half an hour. In her anguish she was determined to leave the next morning come what may. The fact that it would be Christmas Eve made no difference, she would not remain another night under this roof where she had known nothing but unhappiness these past two years.

8

James stared down the empty corridor shaking his head in bemusement. Where had she gone? Had she returned to join the party or retreated to her rooms? What maggot had got into her lovely head to cause her to refuse his offer? Surely she must understand that he had compromised her by kissing her so publicly, by dancing so close together — he would not take no for an answer. He was about to return to the festivities to see if he could find his missing partner when two figures hurried around the corner almost colliding with him. 'Bloomfield, Miss Culley, I had not expected to see you in this part of the house tonight.'

'We have been looking for you, young man, come into the study where we can be private.'

The older man took in the scene at a

glance. 'Good, I hoped this was what you had intended. I offer you my sincere congratulations on your betrothal. Where is Miss Baverstock? I think it would be wise if you kept her close, there's a good deal of unpleasantness heading her way.'

'Elizabeth turned me down, she refused my offer and ran away.'

Miss Culley stared at him through narrowed eyes. 'Did you tell her it wasn't until she appeared in that wonderful gown that you knew you loved her?'

Puzzled by her query he nodded. 'Yes, but how did you know?'

'You have made a sad mull of things, Sir James. Can you not see how Elizabeth would view that statement?'

His heart sank like a stone. 'She believes that I have been bowled over by her appearance, that I do not love her for herself.' He turned away ashamed that he had been so shallow. Elizabeth was correct, he had not thought himself in love when she was plain. It was indeed when her beauty was revealed that he had been prompted to declare himself.

Bloomfield handed him a glass of champagne. 'Drink this, my boy, all may not yet be lost.'

'But she is right, it wasn't until I saw her as she really is that I knew I loved her. I thought my feelings to be that of compassion only.'

'Sir James, tell me honestly, how would you feel if you never saw Elizabeth again.'

'That is an impossibility. However I arrived at this point, one thing I am certain of: I love her and intend to marry her. Nothing and no one shall stand in my way.'

'Excellent, exactly what I hoped you would say. I suggest that you and Bloomfield return to the fray. I shall go up and speak to Elizabeth. Her feelings are deeply wounded, Sir James, I cannot promise she will forgive you right away.'

'As long as she does so eventually, I

shall be content.'

The young lady left him with Bloomfield. 'I have no wish to return to be castigated and criticised. Please, my lord, feel free to go. I intend to remain in here and continue my search of the desk.'

'Actually, Sarah and I have discussed the best way forward. We think it would be helpful if you returned to the ballroom when Sarah gets back from talking to Miss Baverstock.'

James stiffened, he was not accustomed to being told what to do by anyone. He had been his own man since he came down from Cambridge to take over the title and the estates.

'Do not poker up, my boy. Don't you see, if you and Sarah spend time together, those jumped up mushrooms that have inherited this establishment will believe that you were merely flirting with a young lady who was in no position to object.'

'I understand. It will take the attention away from Elizabeth. I have no wish for her to suffer further bullying on my account. I will do it, reluctantly, but I can see the logic behind your notion.'

Whilst they waited for Miss Culley to come back they sat companionably drinking champagne and talking happily about the future when he would be married to Elizabeth and Bloomfield married to Miss Culley.

'Ned and David are taking a grand tour in the New Year. Sarah and I intend to have a quiet wedding in February. Can I ask you to stand up for me?'

'Certainly, if you will do the same when I can persuade Elizabeth to forgive me.'

* * *

Elizabeth hesitated in her dressing room. She was certain she could hear someone moving about in the chamber beyond. Had *he* had the temerity to invade her privacy in this way? Outraged she erupted into the room to find

Sarah sitting on the narrow bed quite happily.

'There you are. I was beginning to think you had got lost in that rabbit warren of passageways out there. I have come with a message from Sir James . . . '

'I have no wish to hear it. He does not truly love me. Like many gentlemen he has let his passions rule his head.'

'My dear, you are quite mistaken. He was maladroit in his proposal but he meant every word he said. Think about it, Elizabeth, could you have fallen head over heels in love with him in less than a day if he had been plain as a pikestaff?'

This put a different aspect to it. If he had been a homely gentleman she might well have come to love him just as much when she had got to know him better, but she would not have succumbed so easily. 'It's quite unfair, Sarah, there must be hundreds of men and women who are not as attractive as they might be, who never find the perfect partner because all the good looking people marry each other. I overreacted, foolishly I turned him down. Will he ever forgive me?'

'He is saying the same thing to Bloomfield at this very moment. It will all come about, you must not fret. When you leave you will be his betrothed, that much is certain.'

Elizabeth danced around the bedroom her happiness restored. Her perambulations ceased abruptly. 'The Hartfords will be so angry. I cannot bear to think what they might say to him on my behalf.'

'We have thought of that. Bloomfield and I think it might be a good idea if Sir James were to pretend he was merely toying with you. I shall dance with him twice and flirt outrageously. If they think you have been slighted they will be more than pleased. With luck they will not pursue the matter further.'

'What does he think of your suggestion?'

'Bloomfield is discussing it now. If

he's prepared to dissemble if it will make life easier for you. I must tell you, my dear, that he is determined to take you with him when he leaves.'

'I had decided to go tomorrow, but that would be silly. James has promised to take care of the staff that are dismissed, but how shall I know who is in need of help?'

Sarah headed for the door. 'I should leave all that to Sir James, he is more than capable of taking care of such things. Did you know that he is not only a baron but also a wealthy man?'

'I don't know whether I'm relieved to hear you say so, as then it will make no difference that I am penniless — or concerned that I am not suitable.'

'Don't be a peagoose, dear girl, your pedigree is better than his. You can hold *your* head up in any drawing-room in England and don't you forget it.'

The door closed and Elizabeth was alone in her bed chamber. She was decidedly hungry. She had fully expected to be eating supper downstairs so had devoured all the food Mrs Blake had brought yesterday. She was reluctant to remove her ball gown, it was the most delectable confection she'd ever owned and she'd been in it scarcely more than an hour. It was far too early to be thinking about retiring. What could she do to while away the time until midnight? It would then be Christmas Eve, the day before the Lord's name day. It was a day when miracles seemed possible, when one could look up into the stars and believe that angels were singing somewhere high above. She had plenty of fuel, she would relight the fires at either end of the schoolroom. After all, she was all but betrothed to a formidable man. He would not let her go cold however long she was obliged to remain at Hartford Hall. If she opened the windows she should be able to hear the music floating up from the ballroom on the ground floor. Even with no Prince Charming to hold her she would dance around the room and relive the magic of the waltz she'd had with James. He was no longer 'Sir James' to her, he was her beloved and in a few weeks time they would be married.

Once the fires were burning brightly and the room warm enough to be comfortable, Elizabeth picked up her skirts and twirled around the room, so happy she thought she might burst from it. Then it was as if a bucket of snow had been tipped over her head. She froze in horror as she remembered that she would not be able to marry without Lord Hartford's permission and he would never give it. She would not be one and twenty until November next year — it was not possible for her to leave with James. An unmarried and unchaperoned young lady could not travel with a gentleman, and she could certainly not live in the same establishment as him. If he were to offer money she would become no better than his mistress, a kept woman. They would both be permanently ostracised from society; it did not matter to her, but she could not put the man she loved in such a position.

Elizabeth ran the golden folds of her gown through her fingers, letting the candlelight play over it. There was only one way around this. She must take up her position as a governess and work with the family until she reached her majority and was free to marry. The problem with this solution was that he would never agree to it, he would try and persuade her that he had no care for society. However, if she left at first light tomorrow as she had planned to do, she would be gone before he missed her. No one knew the location of her employment, she would travel to London and remain in lodgings until the day she was expected. There was a mail coach left from the King's Head at eight o'clock each morning, if she set out at dawn she would be there in good time. As soon as she had completed her packing she would write to James explaining why she'd gone, reassuring him that she loved him and that she would contact him in November. If he still wished to marry her then they could be reunited. It was going to be a long, lonely year for both of them. She would not even have the comfort of receiving his letters — it would be fatal to let him know her whereabouts. He would ride pell-mell to fetch her and that would never do.

Elizabeth pulled the windows closed again. Hearing the music just reminded her what she had lost. It was going to be difficult deciding what to pack, for she could only take what she could carry easily. It was a three mile walk to town and the lane would be slippery and snow-covered. She would pack the essential items first and then see if there was room for any luxuries. Engrossed in her packing she did not hear the schoolroom door opening quietly. The delicious aroma of lobster patties and devilled eggs roused her from her task. She glanced over her shoulder through the communicating door. Her eyes widened as first James, and then Lord Bloomfield, staggered in with laden trays.

'My darling, we could not let you starve in your lonely garret. We have bought you refreshments and wine to drink.' He deposited his burden on the school table and held out his arms. Without hesitation she ran into his embrace. Turning up her face she linked her hands around his neck and waited for his mouth to cover hers. His lips this time were hard and demanding, asking something more from her, telling her how much he loved her. Her blood fizzed around her body, her knees trembled and if he had not been supporting her she would have collapsed in a silken heap at his feet. He raised his head and trailed hot sweet kisses across her cheek and down her neck, she tingled all over not knowing what to expect next. To her disappointment he stepped back smiling down at her with love in his eyes. 'That's enough, my love, we have much to discuss and a delicious supper to share with our friends.'

Only then did she remember that they were not alone. Scarlet from tip to toe she hid her burning cheeks in his cravat. A burst of laughter made her look round in surprise. Then she joined in the merriment; Lord Bloomfield and Sarah had been similarly occupied.

'Quite right, my boy, but food first and talk later. Ladies, if you would like to set out cutlery we shall deal with the wine and lemonade.'

Over supper Sarah told her what had transpired downstairs in her absence. 'Our ploy was successful, Elizabeth, in that it deflected the Hartford's anger from yourself. However, I believe that Sir James is now a social outcast for playing fast and loose with the most popular girl in the neighbourhood.'

'Good gracious, they must think you a hardened rake, James . . . ' Her hands flew to her mouth in horror. It was one thing to use his given name in her own head but quite unacceptable to speak it as she had. 'I beg your pardon Sir James . . . '

'There's no need, sweetheart, I wished you to call me James but thought you might be shocked if I suggested it. From now on you shall be Elizabeth to me as well.'

'I was going to say, James, that you will have all the rackety young widows flocking to your door.'

His eyebrows vanished beneath his hair. 'And what do *you* know, Miss Baverstock, about such matters, might I ask?'

Giggling, she waved airily at him. 'Although I do not go in to society myself I listen to what others tell me and I read the newspapers. There is often interesting gossip to be found on the society pages.'

He shook his head in mock ferocity. 'I am deeply shocked, young lady, that you even know what a rake is.'

She pouted and placed a fingertip on her lips. 'It is a garden instrument, is it not, sir? I must own myself a trifle puzzled as to why a gentleman should be likened to such a thing.'

'You, my angel, are a baggage. Now stop this nonsense, there is something most urgent we must all do.'

Whilst she and James had been talking Sarah and Lord Bloomfield had flung open the windows. The sound of sweet music drifted up through the still night air. He held out his hand and she took it. She was to have the last waltz with the man she loved after all. As they spun in perfect unison he tightened his hold until every inch of her was pressed against his chest. Then, as if she weighed no more than a feather, her feet were floating and he whirled her around with his chin resting on the top of her head. As they turned she saw Sarah as closely held as she, smiling up at her partner, her face illuminated by love.

They were still dancing when they heard the church clock strike midnight. At the last stroke the music stopped and the sound of the cheering and clapping from the guests below filled the room. At this moment Elizabeth knew she could not leave him. Whatever the consequences, she would stay at his side until they could be united in the sight of God.

'Oh dear! I wish I had not eaten quite so much, I feel decidedly queasy after all that spinning around.'

Sarah's laughing comment broke the spell and they each collapsed on to one of the small wooden chairs, once used by children, to catch their breath. Now was the time to tell James the bad news.

'James, I shall not be one and twenty until the end of next November. Lord Hartford will never give me permission to marry. What are we to do?'

'You can elope to Gretna Green and get married over the anvil. I believe it's all the rage amongst the cognoscenti at the moment.'

'We shall do no such thing, Miss Culley. When Elizabeth and I are united it will be with our friends there to wish us well and a sumptuous wedding breakfast to follow. We are not having a havey-cavey ceremony in Scotland.'

How fierce he sounded, but he was quite right. She would hate to be obliged to run away in order to be married. 'Then I have no option but to take up my position as a governess. I cannot live without the benefit of clergy in your establishment, James.'

'You shall do no such thing. You are granddaughter of an earl, it would be most unfitting for you to work for your living. In fact I can safely say it will be over my dead body that you become anyone's companion or governess.'

Lord Bloomfield chuckled and waved his hand for calm. 'Stop bickering, children. I have the perfect solution. You shall come and live with my brood, my dear. No one would ever think me rackety in the slightest.' He winked at Sarah and she blushed rosily.

'Thank you, Lord Bloomfield. If you are sure, I shall be thrilled to come and live with you. I can be companion to your girls whilst you are on your wedding trip.'

'Then everything is settled. We can

spend the next eleven months getting to know each other better. You can choose the furnishings for our home, sweetheart, and maybe I can persuade Lord Hartford to give his consent before the time is up.'

Sarah collected up the dirty crockery and cutlery and placed everything on one tray. 'We had better take this back, I don't want any of the staff to face repercussions in the morning.'

'Don't worry about it, if it goes in the dressing room it won't be seen. I can assure you that none of the items will be missed, there is an over abundance of such things at Hartford Hall.'

Elizabeth and Sarah embraced fondly, his lordship patted her on the cheek affectionately and then they were gone, leaving her alone with James.

'Tomorrow, darling girl, you will be moved downstairs where you belong. You are under the protection of Bloomfield now. In future you will be given the respect you deserve.' He raised her hand and kissed the palm. 'I must not linger here. I shall be counting the minutes until we are together again.'

'Goodnight, my love, take care on the stairs. You had better take a candlestick, the wall sconces will have been doused by now.'

The schoolroom no longer seemed a lonely place. In the past few hours it had been filled with laughter, love and happiness. She spotted the leather folder she'd brought down from the attics. Botheration! She had yet to write a letter to her erstwhile employers saying she was no longer able to take up her position next week. Yawning hugely, she picked up a pen and uncorked the ink bottle. Better to get it done now, she might not have the opportunity tomorrow.

The door crashed open, the ink spilled across the table and Lady Hartford and her daughters stormed in . . .

9

'You are a wanton light-skirt, my girl. You have been up here alone with Sir James these past four hours, I will not have such goings-on under my roof and at Christmas time too.'

Helplessly Elizabeth looked from one face to the other hoping that at least Eleanor would understand, would not condemn her without hearing the true story. Then she realised she could not reveal that Sarah had been up here with Bloomfield, they wished to keep their liaison a secret.

'I shall not lower myself to your level, madam. You may think what you like, your opinion is of no matter to me. Kindly leave my chambers, you are not welcome here.'

'Hoity-toity! Brave words will get you nowhere. You will leave my home right now, miss, I'll not have you soiling my establishment a minute longer.' Lady Hartford turned and beckoned. The two unpleasant footmen who had been outside her door with Lord Hartford edged in. Even they looked shamefaced at what they were being asked to do. 'Take this person to the gates and leave her there. Do it now.'

Eleanor finally spoke up. 'Oh no, please, Mama, you cannot send her out in the middle of the night in a ball gown. She will surely perish from the cold, she does not deserve to die for her misbehaviour.'

'How can you speak up for her, sister? She has betrayed your trust, disgraced our house, is little better than a common . . . '

'Enough, Amelia, hold your tongue. You may collect your cloak and put on your boots, miss. You have five minutes and then you shall be evicted.'

There was no point in arguing, she would do as she was told. Snatching up the precious folder she hurried into her bed chamber. Thank God she had already packed a bag with essentials. She would not arrive at her destination without a change of clothes. There was just time to tear off her gown and pull on her warmest garment. Her cloak was on, her boots laced when her ladyship stormed in.

'Do you come quietly, or do my men have to drag you out like a felon?'

With quiet dignity Elizabeth picked up her carpetbag and walked past her tormentors with head held high. She knew, even if they did not, that she was no longer friendless and destitute. James and Lord Bloomfield would come and find her when they discovered this woman's perfidy. She could hear Eleanor sobbing quietly but did not look back. She needed all her fortitude to get her down the stairs without mishap.

It seemed Elizabeth was not to leave via the front door. She was instead pushed unceremoniously through a rear exit. After the warmth of the house the cold outside took her breath away. She turned to the footmen. 'Release me at once. I have no need of your escort, I am quite capable of walking down the drive myself. And I promise that you will get your comeuppance for your part in this.'

Ignoring the two lackeys Elizabeth strode off into the darkness, not even a glimmer of moonlight to help her see the way. The crunching behind her soon stopped. They had obviously decided she would leave of her own volition and did not need their assistance. No doubt they would be in their beds, snug and warm, before she reached the end of the drive. Even though it was pitch dark the snow glowed strangely and she was able to find her way safely to the gravel drive. She sent up a fervent prayer that she would be able to complete the four mile walk without either falling into a ditch or freezing to death. She stopped for a moment to adjust her muffler so that it obscured her nose and mouth then, with her bag held tightly to her chest beneath the folds of her cloak, she resumed her march.

Several times she stumbled, grazing her hands and knees and dropping her bag. Then as if her prayers were answered, the clouds drifted away leaving the lane bathed in silver light. The church clock struck three times, she had been walking for almost an hour, she should be reaching the outskirts of the town shortly. The Kings Head was her destination. She must not give in to her fatigue or allow the numbing cold to interfere. Somehow she would reach safety, take a room and wait until James came to find her. But her legs were leaden . . . perhaps it would not matter if she rested for a while. She was so tired, a short sleep would restore her and it would be better not to arrive too early at the inn. There was a five barred gate leading to a meadow, set back from the lane. It would be ideal to lean against for a few minutes. Carefully arranging her bag as a cushion, she wrapped her cloak more closely about her person and sank down becoming all but invisible in her hidden corner. It was good to be sitting so comfortably, she could almost imagine she was in front of a roaring fire. It was not nearly so cold as she'd thought. Her eyelids flickered and she fell asleep.

*　*　*

James found his valet snoring quietly in the dressing room and had not the heart to wake him. He could quite easily disrobe himself. Putting his garments on to a convenient chair he climbed into bed, but sleep eluded him. He tossed and turned, heard the clock strike three and decided he might as well get dressed again. His head was buzzing with the amazing possibilities ahead of him. Against all the odds he had finally fallen irrevocably in love with the most wonderful woman. He would no longer be alone, he had someone to share the future with. His mouth curved as he thought how it would feel to hold their first child in his arms.

'Sir James, you should have woken me. Are you getting up or retiring?'

'I could not sleep. I'm going downstairs to find myself a hot drink, why don't you accompany me?' Shrugging on his navy blue, superfine coat he snatched up a starched white band of material and expertly tied his cravat. 'The moon is out. I shall go for a walk whilst you find the kitchens and make me a pot of coffee. Bring it to the study — do you know where that chamber is?'

'I do. Jenny, one of the parlour maids, told me that was where you were yesterday afternoon.'

James threw his caped driving coat over his shoulders and grabbed his gloves and beaver. A candlestick was necessary to see them through the house, but outside would be light enough to walk about without the aid of a lantern. The massive Yule log crackled in the grate, the vestibule was comfortably warm. It made no sense to unbolt the front door. He would find a side exit somewhere and leave that way. The sound of running footsteps behind him made him look round. Was his beloved coming to him? Had she somehow sensed that he was awake?

He waited expectantly, but it was Lady Eleanor who ran down the stairs, her face ravaged by tears. She was still in her evening finery. 'My dear girl, what's wrong? How can I be of assistance?'

'I went to your chamber but you were not in it. Oh, Sir James, a most dreadful thing has happened. My mother has turned Elizabeth out into the night. Amelia told her you and she had spent time alone in her chambers. I did not dare to come and find you until Amelia was asleep. You must go after her, she will likely freeze out there.'

'I thank the good Lord that you have come. Let us pray your intervention has been in time.' Duncan was at his side, his leathery face etched with worry. James turned to him. 'Rouse the house, get all the gentlemen down here. We must start a search. She could be anywhere.' He glared at the shivering girl. 'How long is it since she was turned out?'

'More than an hour, but I persuaded Mama to let her change out of her ball gown. She had warm clothes and boots on.'

'It is a great pity, my lady, that you did not come at once to fetch me. If anything has happened to Miss Baverstock you are as culpable as your mother and sister.'

Duncan ran to the huge brass dinner gong and started hammering on it, an excellent notion. With luck the servants would get up as well. He would not wait, he must set out at once — every minute counted.

'Have the housekeeper prepare a chamber for Miss Baverstock, she will need a roaring fire, hot bricks and warming pans and red flannel. Send the search party after me, I'm going to find a lantern and start looking.'

Outside, every blade of grass, every twig was coated with thick white frost. James's throat ached from the cold and *he* was twice her weight and far more robust. If it was hard for him to breathe, how could someone as frail and delicate as his beloved survive? He hurtled around to the stable yard. He would saddle himself a sturdy horse. When he found Elizabeth he would need to get her back as speedily as possible. James spied the stable bell. It was usually only rung in dire emergencies. He grabbed the rope and swung it vigorously. Two sleep befuddled grooms tumbled down the outside staircase from the loft in which they slept. 'Is there a fire, sir?'

'No. Miss Baverstock has been turned out of the house, she is somewhere in this freezing night. Every moment we waste might prove crucial to her survival.'

Instantly the two men straightened up and within a few minutes they had provided him with a saddled horse, a thick blanket strapped behind the saddle, and a lantern to light his way. They were similarly mounted and, like him, holding a swinging lantern on a pole. They were as grim and tight-lipped as he. He'd overheard their swearing as they gave vent to their feelings. Elizabeth was loved by all who knew her, and these two were as eager to find her as he was. He told them to ride on either side of the drive. He would take the middle path. It was impossible to see her footsteps, the dozens of carriages that had come and gone had all but obliterated the snow. Urging his horse into a trot, he peered from side to side praying he would not see the dark heap of her body lying on the ground.

At the end of the drive he glanced back over his shoulder to see Hartford Hall glowing in the dark. There would soon be more out to help with the search but he would not wait for them, he would push on and pray he could find her first. He pressed on down the narrow lane but found no sign of her. Perhaps he was worrying unnecessarily, and she had managed to walk the four miles and safely reach the town.

'Tell me,' he called out to one of the grooms alongside him, 'where would she go to find shelter?'

Without hesitation the young man replied, 'The King's Head, Sir James. It's a substantial place, the mail coach leaves from there first thing every morning.'

There were small cottages and barns on either side of the lane. It twisted and turned and then broadened and he was in the town itself. 'You take the lead. She must be there. By some miracle she has managed to complete the walk without mishap.'

The place was in darkness, but their lanterns were sufficient to guide them into the yard and to the main entrance. James vaulted from the saddle and banged on the door whilst shouting for attention. As he waited he knew his hope might well be misplaced. It would not take so long for someone to respond if Elizabeth had arrived before him. Eventually the door was pulled open and a rosy cheeked fellow wearing a nightcap peered out.

'Landlord, have you taken in a young woman in the past hour? We have lost Miss Baverstock, she set out from Hartford Hall almost two hours ago and we did not pass her on the road.'

The mention of Elizabeth's name changed the man's demeanour immediately. 'She has not arrived here. God save her, sir, she must still be out there somewhere. I shall rouse my wife and prepare a chamber for her. If she is closer to us than Hartford Hall, bring her here.'

James felt a wave of misery engulf him. He must have ridden past her, she must be lying somewhere in a ditch and he had not noticed. He scrambled back in the saddle and wrenched his horse around. There must be a place he hadn't looked. He kicked his horse into a wild gallop. He remembered they'd passed a five barred gate not more than half a mile away. He'd given it no more than a cursory glance, there was no reason to suppose she would be anywhere but on the lane itself.

He threw himself to the ground and ran into the meadow entrance. At first he saw nothing, then a dark shape huddled in the far corner told him he had found her. He dropped to her side and with shaking fingers placed them under her chin feeling for a pulse. Thank God! She was still alive — but only just. He pushed one arm under her knees, the other around her shoulders and stood up.

The grooms arrived at his side. 'Here, let me help you, Sir James.'

A thick blanket was wrapped around his burden and whilst he scrambled back aboard they held her for him. He leant down and she was carefully handed up to him. He pulled his coat around her. His body warmth might help to keep her alive until he could get her to safety. His willing mount responded magnificently, galloping as easily with a double burden as he had with one. The inn was ablaze with candlelight, the front door wide open, and a plump woman in pristine white apron and cap waited in the flagstone entrance hall to receive him.

'I've sent for the doctor, sir. Bring Miss Baverstock upstairs. You leave her to me and my girls, this won't be the first time we've had to revive a traveller half frozen from the elements.'

James followed her into a substantial chamber. It was almost overpoweringly hot, and two maidservants were busily rubbing warming pans back and forth between the sheets of a huge tester bed.

'Put Miss Baverstock down on the bed, sir. You wait downstairs with Mr Holding, he'll find you a warm drink and something to eat. There's nothing you can do here.'

On impulse he turned and kissed Elizabeth on her blue lips; she was too cold, almost corpse like. If she were to die, his life would be over. He was unceremoniously bustled from the room and had no option but to return downstairs and wait for news. A white hot rage overwhelmed him. That evil woman would pay for this. Whatever the outcome, she would not go unpunished for her cruelty. If his darling girl . . . if Elizabeth should . . . He could not even think of such a thing. His eyes filled, he was unmanned by the tragedy.

'Come along, sir, I have stoked up the fire in a private parlour. There will be hot toddy and meat pasties along in a minute.'

'Thank you, landlord, I am most grateful for your timely assistance.'

He had been sitting nursing a mug of something hot and sweet when Bloomfield threw open the door. 'My boy, what a thing to happen! How is Miss Baverstock, will she do?'

James shrugged helplessly. 'I've no idea. I'm praying for a happy outcome but bracing myself for the worst. She was so cold, so lifeless, I cannot believe she can come back from that.'

The landlord poked his head around the door. 'The doctor is upstairs with Miss Baverstock. My good lady says to tell you things are looking brighter than they were before.'

Bloomfield poured himself a mug of toddy. 'By the by, one of the grooms found a bag. It has gone upstairs, no doubt it has her essentials in it.'

★ ★ ★

Elizabeth was woken by the sound of church bells ringing. Where was she? Were these the bells of heaven welcoming her in?

'My darling, you have come back to me. It has been the longest day of my life. I thought I had lost you. I shall never let you out of my sight again. Hartford will not dare to refuse permission for us to wed, not after this.'

'Are those the bells to welcome in our Lord's birth day? Is it Christmas day already?'

'It is, sweetheart, and the happiest day of my life.'

She still did not know how she had come to be in this strange room, or how he was here beside her and with no sign of any sort of chaperone. 'My love, I can recall nothing after I stopped for a rest. Tell me what happened.'

When he had finished his explanation she settled back on the pillows with a sigh. 'I prayed for deliverance and you were sent to save me. It was a horrible experience but we shall be the stronger for it.' She smiled at him. 'Good gracious! You look like a vagabond, as if it were you that has been sleeping under a hedge, not I.'

He grinned ruefully and rubbed a finger over his dark stubble. 'Now you are awake, I shall leave you for a while and repair my dishevelment. Duncan arrived with my trappings. In fact the King's Head is full to bursting with those that left Hartford Hall on hearing what had happened.'

'Is Sarah here, and Lord Bloomfield?'

He leaned over and dropped a feather like kiss on her lips. 'Indeed, everyone is here, including half your staff who walked out en masse yesterday.'

'But where shall they all sleep? Surely this inn is already full of other guests?'

'No, darling, it's Christmas Day, everyone has gone home to be with their families. We have the place to ourselves. Mrs Blake had the foresight to bring a diligence filled with enough food to feed all of us like kings. She has also brought your belongings and your abigail has sorted them out for you.'

It was midnight. James looked as though he hadn't slept for days; his face was haggard his eyes bloodshot and his complexion pale. 'James, I insist you go at once to your bed. I shall get up in the morning and we can go to matins together. Despite all that has happened it will be the happiest Christmas I've ever experienced because you will be at my side.'

No sooner had the door closed

behind him than she scrambled out of bed in desperate need of the commode. When she was comfortable once more she pushed her feet into her slippers and pulled on her bed-robe. She was wide awake, she could not possibly sleep any more. Good grief! By her reckoning she had been in the land of nod for eighteen hours at least. What could she do to while away the hours until she could ring for her breakfast? The leather folder that had been her grandpa's was on a side table. She would write a letter to the family who had been going to employ her. They would be most displeased at her defection, but must understand that her life had changed and she no longer needed to take up employment of any sort. She frowned. Lord Bloomfield had offered to take responsibility for her upkeep, but surely it wasn't right that a stranger should be obliged to pay for her. Then she remembered what James had said, she would be given permission to marry after all. A warm glow enveloped her at the thought of becoming her beloved's true wife in a matter of weeks. Maybe this time next year she could be holding their first baby in her arms.

Her stomach rumbled loudly. Although there was fresh lemonade in a jug by her bedside, no one had thought to leave her anything to eat. She could hardly go down and look for something herself, and she would not dream of waking any of the staff in the middle of the night. They worked quite hard enough without being obliged to get up and bring her food when they should be asleep. She found paper, ink and quills in a roll-top bureau and sat down to write. For the second time this letter was interrupted by an arrival through her door.

'Good heavens! James, I thought you had gone to your bed. And you have brought me food. I do believe this is becoming a habit of yours.'

He carried the tray over to the table and put it down laughing at her astonishment. '*You* said I was to go to bed, *I* said I was going to shave and change. I knew you must be ravenous, and to tell the truth I have had no appetite today. I have brought chocolate, coffee and a selection of what Mrs Blake thought you might like.'

'Is Mrs Blake up as well?'

His arms encircled her and he gathered her close. 'No one was able to sleep until you were out of danger. Everyone is now enjoying a midnight feast. When we have done I promise I shall go to my chamber and get some rest.'

She snuggled into his embrace where she felt safe, warm and protected. She would never be mistreated again. Between them they demolished the contents of the tray and he carefully stacked the remnants and dirty utensils and placed it outside the door for collection.

'This is a handsome object, my love, where did you come by it?'

He was holding the leather folder. 'I discovered it in my grandfather's old bureau. It had been in his bed chamber but on her arrival Lady Hartford banished it to the attic along with the rest of his belongings.'

Idly he flicked it open. His eyes widened and he drew a thick sheet of parchment from the inside. He held it out so she could read the inscription.

The last will and testament of Lord Edward Hartford, Earl of Stoke.

The missing will had been found at last.

'James, can we open it? Is it lawful for us to read this document or should we wait for the lawyers to come?'

He brought it to her and placed it in her hands. 'You read it, my love. I'm sure it will put matters right. I cannot believe your grandfather would have left you unprovided for.'

Her fingers were trembling. It was difficult to break the seal and smooth the thick, cream paper out. He fetched a candelabra and by this added light she perused the contents. Surely not? She had expected something, but never this.

'What is it, sweetheart? Tell me.'

Speechless she handed the document to him. She watched his expression as he read, but unlike her he was not shocked. With a triumphant shout he swept her up into his arms and swung about like a child.

'It is true justice. I had thought the estate and money must be entailed, it never occurred to me that it was only the title your grandfather could not control. You are a very rich woman. Everything is yours! The Hartford's get nothing but the title, they must vacate the Hall immediately and return from whence they came.'

'Put me down, James. I need time to take this in. We can all return, my staff do not have to leave after all. However, I shall not throw the Hartfords out on Christmas Day. They may remain there until the 27th of December. That should give them time enough to pack and make arrangements.'

'After what they did to you I should not have blamed you if you had treated them to a taste of their own medicine. Tomorrow I shall ride up there with this document and set things in motion.' He smiled his toe-curling smile before continuing softly, 'This changes everything. You are now a great heiress, and will be the most sought-after young lady in the country. Do you still wish to marry someone so far beneath you?'

She pouted provocatively and peeked at him through lowered lashes. 'I don't know, Sir James. Perhaps I shall jilt you and hang out for a duke.'

'Over my dead body. As I have told you once before, my darling, you are an unprincipled baggage.'

He put his arms around her and she relaxed against him with a happy sigh. There had been a fairytale ending after all.

THE END

We do hope that you have enjoyed reading this large print book.

Did you know that all of our titles are available for purchase?

We publish a wide range of high quality large print books including:
Romances, Mysteries, Classics
General Fiction
Non Fiction and Westerns

Special interest titles available in large print are:
The Little Oxford Dictionary
Music Book, Song Book
Hymn Book, Service Book

Also available from us courtesy of Oxford University Press:
Young Readers' Dictionary
(large print edition)
Young Readers' Thesaurus
(large print edition)

For further information or a free brochure, please contact us at:
Ulverscroft Large Print Books Ltd.,
The Green, Bradgate Road, Anstey,
Leicester, LE7 7FU, England.
Tel: (00 44) **0116 236 4325**
Fax: (00 44) **0116 234 0205**